*'He is a day-dreamer who works far
too slowly'*   Technical Drawing, Mr Grant

What a life! I woke up at half-past seven all
washed up like a piece of rubbish in the
Severn mud . . . Who said it was a dog's life?
A schoolkid's life is far worse and when you
get a bad report, everything's three times as
bad.

Also available from
Michael Pearson

Winners and Losers
The Bubble Gum Champion

MICHAEL PEARSON

Oh, That Sinking Feeling

Teens · Mandarin

First published 1987
by Methuen Children's Books
This edition first published
under the title *Splashers* 1987
reissued 1989 by Teens · Mandarin
Michelin House, 81 Fulham Road, London SW3 6RB
Copyright © 1987 Michael Pearson
Printed in Great Britain
by Cox & Wyman Ltd, Reading

ISBN 0 416 07532 0

Contents

1. My Stroke of Genius, nearly   9
2. In the Swim of Things, so to speak   19
3. Chico Starts the Ball Rolling, almost   29
4. Marathon Men, and Women!   36
5. Minor Reprimands, but Major Rivals   44
6. Cricket the Money-spinner?   51
7. Ruthie's Super-Disco, and How I Saved the Day   60
8. Treasure-hunting, sort of   70
9. Catching Some Crooks!   77
10. The Escape   88
11. A Helping Hand Gets Bitten   97
12. The Great Swanswell Auction   105
13. Calling it Quits, or trying to   118
14. Trouble-makers!   126
15. The Swanswell Street Theatre   134
16. Many Happy Returns   148
17. Jackpot! (At last)   156
18. The Nastiest of Video Nasties   167
19. An Unexpected Withdrawal   179
20. The End of a Song and Dance   184

'Benevolence is difficult!'
   Confucius

'Doing good is the truest happiness that the human heart can enjoy.'
   Rousseau

1. My Stroke of Genius, nearly

'It is time he put his intelligence and initiative to good use' Mr R. Thorne, Head

It was the second day after my report, and day two of the New Era. Even though it was a fine summer morning with the sun beaming gently down on the woods and fields, it was great to be in school. The glass door of the Technical Drawing room was open and so were all the windows. In fact old Granite, I mean Mister Grant, was such an excellent teacher that he'd opened them before we'd even arrived for the lesson so that his dear little room was cool as well as quiet.

They're right you know, I told myself repeatedly, school days are the best days of your life. It was such a great place to be. If it wasn't for school I'd by lying in the shade of a tree getting eaten alive by horse-flies and midges, or catching diseases and cutting my feet in the cool waters of the Pill. But no, I was preparing myself nobly for lots of good 'O' levels, 'A' levels, University and thousands of pounds a year in the job that had better be waiting for me when I'd finished.

Outside, I saw Watson driving the old lawn mower, with his dog sitting beside him to make sure he knew where to mow.

As the engine spluttered to a halt, the dog jumped down and raced around inspecting the mechanism while Watson poked wearily about. Then with a rattle and another roar it started again, the dog leapt with spring-loaded legs on to the seat and Watson climbed up obediently beside him.

9

Soon the Technical Drawing room was full of the mower's roar, growing fainter as it rumbled down the field and the smell of fresh-cut grass wafted sweetly in. I . . .

'DUCKER!'

Mr Grant, greatly concerned at my momentary loss of interest in the subject he worshipped, got to his feet. I returned earnestly to my task. I was quite good at Technical Drawing. All you needed was a sharp pencil and skill with a rubber.

'That's all very neat,' he pointed out behind my right shoulder, 'but not very accurate is it? If a carpenter tried to build it the way you've drawn it, the whole thing would collapse on the floor. Now concentrate!'

'Yes sir,' I obeyed, grateful for being corrected. And so I concentrated till the end of the lesson. Fortunately we still had fifty minutes left.

The bell went for break, and so did everybody else. We had Maths afterwards and then Spanish. Two of my favourite lessons. Well, I liked them all actually.

During break I spotted the smokers behind the science labs: Chico, Maria Kelly, the Burroughs gang, Barnsie and a couple of others. A small cluster of nasty coughs and nervous glances. With a sniff of disgust at the strength of human weakness I walked to the other end of school.

Ruth Pendryll, the vicar's daughter, was having an early bite of her lunch with Dawn Devonshire, a farmer's gorgeous offspring, standing tupperware to tupperware. Dawn was just popping a curly crisp into her delicious lips.

'Remember what Stoney, I mean Mr Stone, said,' I reminded them. 'Vitamin C. Lots of fruit and no crisps or chocs.'

Dawn took some orange peel out of her lunch box and promptly stuffed it into my shirt pocket, smiling sourly.

'Put that in the bin on your way back, there's a good sucker, Ducker!'

'Of course, Dawn,' I replied politely. After all, it would be a terrible thing if our lovely school were to be soiled by litter. A great shame I was the only one who thought so.

I lay down on the grass a few feet from where the girls had sat down and listened to their twittering conversation about late swallows.

'Look, there's one!' shrieked Ruth suddenly and leapt to her feet pointing at the blue sky. They had both been concerned about not seeing any swallows. They didn't like me explaining it was due to Italian hunters shooting them all for supper. Now, both girls were on their feet, would you believe, waving at this bird, a dot in the sky, twisting and flittering above them.

'Ah, but you know what they say,' I pointed out. 'One swallow does not make a lot of swallows. . . .'

They gave me a dirty look each and sat down again. As I lay basking in the sun I had this strange feeling. Just one more thing was needed to make this place perfect. As I lay back gazing at the empty sky it came to me straight out of the blue.

'A swimming pool! That's what we need. A swimming pool!'

I jumped up, looked round and raced off after the two girls who had wandered off during my daydream.

'A swimming pool?' sneered Ruth. 'What on earth do we want a pool for?'

'But think of it, Ruthie,' I told them and gazed warmly at Dawn who seemed to like the idea. 'Hot, sunny, summer days and the nearest pool is Dursley, and . . . also. . . .'

This new idea was making me weak at the knees. Dawn waited. 'Just think, Dawn . . . you could . . . er . . . wear your bi-bikini.'

'I don't have a bikini, Ducker,' she informed me. 'But our neighbours do have their own pool. Their eighteen-year-old son has promised to invite me over when it's really warm enough.'

And with that they both strolled away up the field to creep to Miss Bleach, who was on eagle-eyed duty that morning, and blow on her coffee for her. Miss B. wouldn't care for a swimming pool unless we let her walk on the water. She taught Humanities and Religious Education and thought old Thornie, our Headmaster was a 'truly wonderful man', much to his embarrassment.

Obviously I would have to try somewhere else. In the Youth Centre yet another of Murphy's 'heavy metal' cassettes was rocking the rafters of the leaky terrapin. When it had finished I rushed forward with the good news.

'Lads, I have just had an ace brainwave. A really brill idea!' I shouted. Murph pushed me gently to one side and put some chalk on his cue. The black was right by the pocket but hugging the cushion. He bent down low, taking aim, chin on cue.

'A swimming pool! Eh? Yeah, that's right – a pool! Magic idea, eh lads? Tell me I'm a genius and I won't deny it this time.'

I wasn't getting too much attention so I slammed the table in triumph. Murphy's cue ball shot across the table and socked the pocket. The black eased itself slowly away from the cushion. Murph was a statue.

'Thanks, Murph!' laughed Rich Streeter, who should have really been swotting for his 'O' levels. All three of them.

'Thanks, Ducker,' Murphy growled and used the butt end of his cue to prod me down the room towards the dart board.

'But a pool, Murph – think of it. Just what we want.'

'Kids' game,' he grunted, turning his broad back on me. Typical Murph, I thought. Meanwhile Davy Cole was throwing his first dart. It hit the tyre. He may have been my best mate but he was a lousy dart player.

'Surely, Davy, you must realise what a good idea a swimming pool is.'

'If I fancies a dip, Ducker, I goes in the canal,' he told me cheerfully and threw his second dart. It bounced off and landed point down in Noddy Bright's foot.

'You're not supposed to though,' I put in. 'Anyway, the pool won't be polluted for one thing.'

Noddy's one-footed war-dance hopped round in a vicious circle as Davy grinned.

'Depends who uses it.' And with that he screwed up his face like toothache to concentrate. He stood up, glared at Noddy for a second, waited till the screaming stopped and threw his last dart. It actually landed on the board, but the wrong side of the wire. Minus a hundred and eighty!

I instructed him about his technique, told him he should rest his elbow on his paunch and left him with a bag up his jumper trying it out. As the shouts of 'double top!' echoed round the terrapin I strolled out thoroughly dejected and tottered down the steps. No one was interested in my brilliant scheme. One of the girls had suggested I saw Des, our new youthleader, about it. He was always full of bright ideas on how to improve the school.

Suddenly, to my right, there were shrieks and shouts of terror and panic. The smokers, all seven of them, led by Chico raced across the yard, knocking over a couple of first year tots and the empty school dustbin.

'Chico – what about a swimming pool?' I yelled after him as he sprinted down the yard by the gym and skidded round the corner. As I turned away, Thornie, the man himself, came walking slowly and thoughtfully from the science labs writing something in a notebook. Then, at last the bell went.

As a last resort I walked beside my trusty leader all the way to the doors of the yard and the freshly-formed queue. First I wished him a polite good morning. Then:

'Sir, have you ever considered what a difference a swimming pool would make to the life of the school?'

Still sticking close and ignoring his grunt of 'No', I

ambled past the long line of mutinous mutterers, through the door and down the corridor. I continued.

'In summer for instance. Everybody could use it. Adults and children. Primary schools could pop in during the day. You could keep it open after school, even during holidays. You'd have to charge then, of course. But you'd not only make lots of money, you'd be the centre of everything. The school would be the local main attraction, sort of. . . .'

By the time I'd got this far we were in the foyer by the office. He'd been trying hard to shrug me off with a few more 'Nos,' and 'Now what are you up tos,' but he suddenly stopped, gave me a strange stare and repeated dreamily: 'The main attraction? The centre of the community? Ah . . . yes. . . .'

He snapped out of it and looked down at me as if I'd changed from a frog to a prince. 'Why has no one else thought of this?' he asked.

'I don't know, sir,' I replied with princely modesty.

'And where are we going to get the money from?' he asked widening his eyes meaningfully.

I repeated, 'I don't know, sir,' even more modestly.

'And do you know how much a swimming pool would cost us?'

'A lot, sir?' I suggested, guessing at the princely sum.

'A lot more than that,' he concluded and I became a frog once more.

'But sir . . .' I croaked as he strode away down his corridor. 'We could have a go ourselves, sir – the kids I mean . . . .'

He was just about to kick me back to my maths lesson, when the idea started to interest him again. He smiled grimly and nodded.

'I appreciate why you're trying to do all this, but I think you are being far too ambitious. Yet, if you could get it off the ground; well, put it this way: if the school could raise the first thousand, I'll squueze the rest out of parents and others. You see, I do like the idea, Ducker. I'd like it to work . . . if it's possible. . . .'

At last. It was a deal. He stuck out his hand and for a moment I thought it was to shake mine, but instead he clenched it and pointed the index finger over my head back down the corridor. 'Maths.'

When I told Stoney, our tutor, during afternoon registration he seemed delighted. 'Excellent idea – I'll give you all Tutor Period tomorrow to tell the class about it. You can make it last fifteen minutes, can't you?'

I must admit, I was so excited and inspired by the brilliance of my own genius that I had to concentrate really hard on the afternoon's lessons. All too soon the final bell of the day came and I packed my Gola bag sadly, ready for my mournful journey home. Still, never mind, there was always homework.

I arrived back at the pub at four o'clock. Mum was in the kitchen swotting up for the 'A' level. She was reading a book called *A Farewell to Arms* which made me think of a statue of Venus. As I was thinking this unusual thought she glanced up.

'Much homework?' she asked sharply. I nodded eagerly and smiled. 'Better get started then!'

And off I trotted. Upstairs in the main bedroom was a dead body with a bee up its nose, as Dad continued his afternoon nap.

I looked at my homework schedule. A drawing of an artesian well, a chapter of the latest book Mrs Potter was boring the pants off us with and ten words of Spanish.

At half-past four, I drew the line under my pretty picture. Dad, all flushed and pumped up with sleep, stood sleepily in my doorway.

'Much homework?' he grunted sadly. I nodded and reached for part two. He disappeared in the gloom of the landing. I copied out the ten Spanish words on to a piece of paper, stuffed it in my back pocket, walked to the cupboard, picked up the stump and the ball and tiptoed down into the garden. Dad was blundering about in the cellar, falling over crates and Mum was still doing her homework, so I'd be all right for half an hour at least.

I hammered the stump into the usual spot and took eleven paces back. Then put a lollystick down for my mark. I started off with a couple of out-swingers, good ones too, and got down then to the serious business of perfecting my leg-cutters. As the swingers started to weave through the air, I began to relax and almost feel a sense of real achievement.

It was the end of the day, but I still had a few problems. Not schoolwork; I'd been a good boy all day. Not homework; I'd finished that. I would read the book in bed and learn the words while I was bowling round the wicket. No, my problem was a thousand pounds, worse than any of these. Somehow I'd have to persuade the four hundred and twenty kids of Swanswell Comprehensive that a swimming pool was something worth raising a thousand pounds for. So far the only person really interested was Thornie; and though he must have been filthy rich, what with his headmaster's salary and everything, I couldn't see him being that generous ever.

However, bowl by bowl, the ideas started coming to me. All I had to do was persuade 3L, then the rest of the school would follow; even the sixth form. We were the most dynamic class in the school once we got going and thought positive. But we needed winding up before we got going. My little talk tomorrow would have to be good.

'I have a vision: a vision of hot, dry and dusty summer days. I have a vision of cool, blue waters waiting to be dived in. . . .'

That sounded fair enough.

'Cool blue waters where every boy and girl in Swanswell can take a dip without taking a long, hot trip. Yes, for while the rest of the world has to trek off to Gloucester and Dursley, we at Swanswell merely pop into school, because there will be a pool; yes a pool waiting for one and all. . . .'

Apart from the rhymes it was sounding really great.

'But, this is not a vision, or a dream it's a. . . .'

'OWIZZEE?'

I jumped a foot in the air as this voice jeered over the hedge. It was Gary Streeter on his ten speed. He had his light blue tee-shirt on with one of his medallions bouncing off his broad, weightlifted chest.

'Gary, my old he-man. Have you ever fancied yourself as a lifeguard?' I asked, retrieving the ball. He ought to have, he fancied himself as everything else. I elaborated for him as his mouth hung open and his eyes went all dreamy.

'I mean, supposing we had a swimming pool in our school. You just think; you could be a life-guard showing off your latest muscles to all the crumpet. . . .'

'You've noticed my pectorals then?' he interrupted and, leaning his bike against the hedge, he took a deep breath and turned his arms inwards like trophy handles. 'Starting to get definition already; only been working the weights for six weeks, too.'

'Pectorals?' I gasped. 'What are they?'

'Chest muscles, you berk,' he said tersely. 'Now what d'you think of the definition?'

'I dunno,' I shrugged. 'Chest muscle's as good a definition as any.'

'No, no, the definition of the muscles, you know.'

He started to pump up his biceps next and sniffing them, first right then left.

'Well, Ducker, what d'you think?' What was I supposed to say?

'You'll be the best-looking life-guard for miles around,' I

reassured him. He pulled a face. He turned slowly, his arms still up in the air like a crab.

'What's this life-guard crap you keep on about? We ain't got no swimming pool.'

'Ah no, my muscle-bound mate, not yet, but . . .' I was just going to tell him of my vision and rope in my first recruit when my window flew open, a sharp voice called my name and Mum shouted:

'I thought you said you had lots of homework,' so that all the world and the Forest of Dean could hear. 'You know what your report said.'

Gary was just loving this. He laughed. 'Aha – you bad boy, Ducker! Get back in there and finish your homework. You know what your report said.'

Yes, I knew what my report said. It was the worst report ever written in the History of the Western World. But I'd sworn to change. I'd been a good boy for two whole days. Forty-eight flipping hours. The longest two days of my little life!

2. In the Swim of Things, so to speak

*'He is a day-dreamer who works far too
slowly'*   Technical Drawing, Mr Grant

What a life! I woke up at half-past seven all washed up like
a piece of rubbish in the Severn mud. I'd had that dream
again. There I am in this huge swimming pool, ten times
larger than the one in Gloucester. I'm standing pressed
close to the tiled wall, hanging on to a handrail for dear life.
Suddenly, the floor starts to tilt down towards the water.
The handrail comes away from the wall and I pitch
screaming into the thick green scummy liquid. I sink below
the surface but I can see all these kids, faces I recognise,
lining up at the edge of the pool, pointing down at me and
laughing. Down and down I sink into the inky-blue depths.

Still shuddering from the after-effects of a bad night's
sleep, I trudged through the school gates. Watson and his
clockwork dog came whirring along. They were off to mark
out the field for the athletics match tonight. Who said it was
a dog's life? A schoolkid's life is far worse and when you get
a bad report, everything's three times as bad. They went on
and on at me:

'I find this report a big disappointment for several
reasons,' growled Stoney the morning after they'd been
dished out. 'You're too intelligent to get reports like this.'

'You realise you've let everybody down,' rumbled
Thornie, that same afternoon. 'You've let down the school,
your parents, but most of all – yourself.'

'You do realise you've let us down,' remarked my mother
sharply, that same evening.

'You know, this won't do at all,' mumbled Dad, an hour after Mum's interrogation. 'We all thought you'd do so well here. And yet, look at this; they all say the same: "Has ability but makes no effort. Too easily distracted" etc, etc.'

The kids weren't quite so critical. 'Nice one, Ducker!' congratulated Chico during the next morning's break, offering me a soggytip behind the labs. 'And welcome to dossers' corner. We're just practising our poses for the dole queue. . . .'

However, there was one exception. 'Oh honestly, Ducker!' shrieked Ruthie Goodie-Two-Shoes at the end of the same break. 'You're just a pathetic joke! I thought you had brains! I thought you had principles! I thought you were different!'

God knows what she thought I was. There was a time when she fancied me like mad: I even went out with her a couple of times – quite nice times, except that she never stopped talking. But I soon realised she wasn't madly in love with me, but what she could make out of me; wanting to model me into the perfect person. Once I failed to make the grade and insisted on being plain ordinary Ducker, that was it. She had been gunning for me every since.

I could have put the blame on somebody else perhaps: living in a pub, girls, Chico, Jammy, the comprehensive system, the Government, but in the end I said nothing, except 'sorry'. So here we are: Jammy, my violinist friend, is now safe out of harm's way in another class and for two days I've stayed out of trouble and conned myself that I love school and everything connected with it. But I really did want to get that swimming pool built, whatever the others thought.

Stoney beckoned me to the front of the class and to my horror instead of hushing them up, said, 'All yours,' and started to sort out books and boxes in the farthest corner of the room.

I stood there listening to the lads chat and the girls gossip and the rabble gabbling about nothing in particular.

'Ahem! I, er . . . have this vision, you know, a sort of idea that I got yesterday morning,' Chatter-chatter, rabble-gabble.

'Listen then – I have a vision of, er . . . what we could really do with. . . .' Chat-chat; gossip-shop; rabble-gabble.

'I reckon we really need. . . .' Rabble-gabble. 'For crissake will you lot shuddup and listen!'

Silence. For three seconds. 'Yeah Ducker, we know about you and your swimming pool!'

'Daft idea! Boring! Who needs one? Siddown! You'll be sorry!' And the rabble-gabble erupted, twice as loud as before.

At last, Stoney, trying not to laugh all over his horrible hairy mug, comes down the front, faces the mob and raises his paw. 'All right, that will do.' Instant silence. What it is to be feared! He told the quiet class that he'd like to hear what I had to say and thought they ought to listen. Anyway, with sir's help, I was doing quite well until I got to the words 'thousand pounds'. Then they were at it again: whooping, whistling, rolling their eyes, laughing and falling silent the minute Stoney raised both paws.

Chico put up his hand, obviously coming to my rescue. 'Tell me Ducker – can you swim?'

'Er, no . . .' I stuttered and went red. They all jeered again. 'But. . . .'

'So what d'you want a swimming pool for?' another voice asked.

'Creeping to Thornie after his bad report, that's why.'

Dawn raised her lily-white arm. 'I say we all offer to help Ducker . . . only after he learns to swim, and not before.'

The class all brayed their agreement and nodded their donkey heads at me. Stoney, my favourite teacher now, came to my assistance once more and suggested that all those who were genuinely interested in helping raise the money should stay behind for a few minutes, so I could get a list of names.

And what a list! All five of them. And what five: Bonehead Wilkins, with his finger up to the knuckles in his left nostril; Beryl and Cheryl, the twins; Noddy Bright and, of course, Davy Cole.

'Any ideas then?' I grunted, ready to give in and pack the whole thing up. Noddy raised his hand like he was in class.

'Yeah; g-go treasure huntin'. Me and my C-Scope. We keeps finding valuable stuff all over the place, all of the time.'

I sagged in despair. Noddy and his C-Scope mine-sweeper were the joke of the whole school. But not the biggest joke. No, the biggest joke was Ducker's Swimming Pool; or rather non-swimming pool.

Having stabbed me nicely in the back, Chico had the nerve to come up and offer to help me out of my dilemma.

'It's no good, Ducker,' he said with a wise shake of his treacherous head in the youth centre. 'You'll just have to learn to swim.'

'But I've been trying for years,' I yelled. He stepped back amazed.

'What's been the problem then?'

'I've been too scared to go in the water.'

There was no way they were going to bully me into going into any of that lethal liquid. Murph looked up from his latest snooker disaster. 'How deep's this pool going to be, Ducker? Two inches in the shallow end and three inches in the deep end, eh?' Roars of laughter all round. Maybe learning to swim wasn't such a bad idea.

Chico sensed my change of attitude and took me to one side. He produced a pound from his back pocket.

'Ducker, I will bet you a shiny golden quid that I can teach you to swim, not in years, not in days – but in minutes!'

'Minutes? Oh yeah?' I wailed scornfully as he winked and

tapped the side of his nose. But one thing about Chico, he's a real little dynamo. Once he winds you up, off you go.

Saturday morning I was shivering in my trunks at the banks of the Pill. The deep part.

It was quite a warm day and the branches of the trees waved gently over the bank. Further upstream some unsuspecting boys were fishing and Benny McMenemy was kneeling at the edge trying to catch shrimps in a yellow plastic bowl. He was bent over it like a prospector panning for gold.

'Any luck, Ben?' I shouted, trying to change the subject. He didn't answer. I had a long look round: what with the slow-moving river, and the meadow and the banks and trees, everything was a soft, peaceful green – just like the last view of the drowning man!

All the kids in the village had turned up to see this great spectacle, hadn't they? Davy, Beryl and Cheryl, numerous tots and Gary Streeter in his gold briefs, who soon started feeling my muscles, or rather, looking for them.

'Blimey, Ducker, my biceps are bigger than your thighs,' he announced in amazement. The fact that my biceps were bigger than his brains had to stay a secret for the moment because Chico pushed his way through the giggling crowd carrying an enormous black rubber ring; a car tyre's inner-tube.

'Make way for the star please, come on, give him some room,' he began and they all stood back, gawping twice as much as Chico, with the gentlest of shoves, guided me to the very edge of the bank. Then he handed me the tyre, which felt quite solid and comforting. I squeezed it tightly and something squeaked in my ear.

'Er . . . now what?' I stammered, shivering even more violently. There was a snigger of pleasure and anticipation among the spectators.

23

'I'm going to give you the swimming lesson, that's what,' he explained. 'So, now jump in . . .'

'Jump? But this is the deep bit!'

'And you've that ginormous ring, so jump in!'

My mouth was still open in protest as his extra hard shove sent me tottering over the edge of the bank and kicking the air into the water. My body jerked back to the surface immediately as I gritted my teeth, petrified, and clutched that ring for dear life. This was worse than any nightmare. But the ring held firm and I floated safely on the water, spat out a mouthful of bilge at a couple of water boatmen and wondered what that funny squeaking noise was.

'OK, Ducker?' called Chico through cupped hands as I floated towards the centre. 'Now get those legs kicking. That's it. Good strong kicks.'

'Big deal,' I muttered as I got those legs kicking. This wasn't swimming, this was splashing water. Then I began to cheer up as it seemed that the shiny, golden quid was as good as mine.

'Now then, Ducker. Listen carefully. The Chico Marks speedy swimmer course, stage one,' he called out as the spectators clapped.

'Ready?' I echoed his question.

'Now, Ducker, that ring you're holding on to for dear life. . . .'

'Ye-es?' I blurted out as the speaking got louder.

'It's got a puncture. And you've got about thirty seconds left. So start swimming.'

It was quite a clever idea I suppose, even if it didn't work. Seconds later I was back on shore with Gary pummelling my shoulder blades and Chico shaking his head at a rare failure.

'You let me down, Ducker,' he complained, using my favourite phrase. 'It's worked loads of times before.'

'Yeah,' added Gary in disgust. 'What you want to start that screaming for? I was dead embarrassed.'

'Oh, I don't know,' I spluttered, coughing up crabs. 'Maybe I was somewhat apprehensive, even slightly concerned about drowning. You get like that when you're a non-swimmer in ten-flipping-feet of water, thank you very much!'

'Never mind, Ducker,' Davy giggled, as Beryl and Cheryl helped me cautiously to my feet. 'I'll teach you next time.'

I dusted the twins off, grabbed a towel and marched off after Chico, hand held open.

'One pound!' I pointed out.

Him pay me? I must have been joking. Oh no, he said he'd teach me to swim in minutes, but he didn't say which minutes.

'You know, Chico, you're a real friend,' I cussed him. 'First you ruin my swimming pool enterprise, then you try to drown me, now you cheat me out of a quid!'

And I turned and walked away. He looked startled and quite upset about it and raced after me.

'Tell you what, Ducker, I'll bet you another shiny, golden quid—'

'Forget it. I am not interested.' A procession of little kids was following us along the bank.

'No, wait,' he shrieked. 'I bet you a quid I'll be able to sell your swimming pool idea to 3L!'

'Done!' He nearly ran into me as I span round with outstretched hand. This was more like it. If anybody could wind up 3L he could. He could talk the hind legs off two donkeys. We were quits.

'But you know what they said,' he grinned craftily. 'No one moves until you learn to swim.'

I didn't need reminding. He sort of leaned back and sized me up. 'Let me have another go. I promise you won't let me down. . . .'

'Oh no.'

'The Chico Marks Special Swimming Course . . . er . . . stage two. This one. . . .'

'No chance.'

'Honest, Ducker, it's much easier,' he called after me, as I marched off down the path clutching my towel and still wearing my wet trunks, of course. 'It's a lot safer too.' His voice grew faint. 'All you do is put on a pair of loose flippers. . . .'

I was trapped. Nobody would lift a finger to help me until I could swim, thanks to Chico and Dawn. By the time I did learn to swim, if Chico hadn't drowned me in the process, we'd have all left Swanswell and be on the dole.

As I wandered sadly out of the meadow and strolled to the bridge, Davy Cole rode after me on his bike. He'd teach me how to swim, he reckoned. He promised. One thing about Davy, he was one of those rare human beings who was true to his word. He'd seen it done on telly, in a Tarzan film, which was very reassuring, I must say. But by now I was desperate.

Next morning I was there again, only at the part of the Pill that wasn't so deep. The crowd had doubled.

'This had better work, Davy,' I warned him, stepping into the shallow water by the trees. 'If my old dear ever founds out, we're both dead!'

'Quit moaning and grab hold of this,' he commanded and chucked me the floppy end of a long piece of rope. I hate to admit it, but I was wearing his sister's water wings.

I flapped and splattered towards the centre of the Pill once more, where it was only five feet deep, grabbed the rope tight and a whole line of kids started to heave it along the bank, while Davy shouted at me to kick my legs.

'Right, now without the stupid water wings,' he ordered after about ten minutes of heaving and kicking.

'Couldn't we do without them next week?'

26

'Don't be such a fairy, Ducker. Now, when we pull you kick like mad!'

The Volga boatmidgets started to haul me through the shallow bilge. I straightened out and began to kick feebly. As the taunts from the bank increased, so I kicked more powerfully. It worked. At least I was afloat. But worse was to come.

'Now Ducker – let go the rope and paddle with your hands.'

No chance. I kicked and clung on tight as they heaved me well and truly into deep water. Soon everybody was shouting and screaming at me to drop the rope. Next Saturday, I remember thinking, till Gary stepped forward and with one almighty yank wrenched it out of my hands.

I heard a gasp from the bank. I saw Davy's eyes pop out of his head in horror at his folly. I saw Gary perch at the edge with his arms out straight, ready to dive in and fetch me, again. Then, he dropped his arms, stepped back, tapped Davy's shoulder and pointed at me. Davy, I noticed, was smiling. Next thing I knew they were all cheering and repeating this strange little phrase, 'Ducker can swim!'

I felt like a real hero after having swum at least seven strokes. I waded out dripping with glory. It was dead easy really, swimming. If you can get everything that moves to splash at the same time for long enough you're bound to stay afloat sooner or later.

'That was the most pathetic dog-paddle I've ever seen,' commented Gary. 'Still, better than nothing. What gets me, though, is why you have to scream like that. . . .'

'Well I didn't know I could swim,' I explained. 'Pity Dawn wasn't here to see it.'

'Oh yeah,' giggled Davy. 'She'd be very impressed. Watching you scream and do dog-paddle, then see your weedy body when you get out.'

Davy, my wiry, blond-haired mate, could insult me as much as he liked now. I owed him a lot. Thanks to him and Tarzan, I could now swim and was ready to launch the great Swanswell Swimming Pool Appeal.

3. Chico Starts the Ball Rolling, almost

'A friendly member of the class who must try and keep out of bad company'   Mr M. J. Stone, Tutor

'Do I have to, Ducker?' Chico whines on the way into the drama hall that Monday for Ducker's Special Assembly. I reminded him that it was either that, or two shiny, golden quids.

After the chattering, gossiping rabble had shambled in and sat on the carpet, Badger, our head of year, introduced me to introduce Chico. And off he went.

'Right. Let's get a few things straight, shall we? I'm not standing up here in front of you lot 'cos Ducker's lost his bottle and can't face you lot after the bird 3L gave him on Thursday. I'm here 'cos I like the idea, believe it or not, and want to sell it to anyone who listens.'

They listened, and there was a rustle of interest and approval. He turned and winked at me.

'Now some of you – like the whole of 3L – reckon Ducker only wants us to have this swimming pool because he had a bad report and sees this as his big chance to creep to Thor . . . I mean Mr Thorne. Which may be true – but never mind Ducker, what about you lot? Think what a swimming pool means to you. Right? It's a hot sunny day, you're all sweaty and pong like an Australian rugby team and want to cool off somewhere. But where? The canal? With all those pleasure boats charging up and down it these days? The Pill? There's not much of that left after Ducker drank three-quarters of it over the weekend. The baths in Gloucester – full of dirty bodies who only bath in summer and guess where? No, no. But imagine we have a swimming pool here, right here in Swanswell. Blimey, it'll be better than Butlins!'

All eyes were on Chico, even the teachers were awake during this assembly.

'Oh, so suddenly you wouldn't mind a pool in school? Well, nor would I. But what about the money, I hear you all shriek? No problem, 'cos old Thor . . . Mr Thorne also likes the idea, which is good news for Ducker's next report maybe, and good news for us, because he's arranged it so that we only have to raise a mere thousand quid and the parents do the rest. I say we start today. . . .'

He made as if to sit down, as if it was all over. But he'd noticed the shuffle and groan at the magic number. So he did a shimmy and stepped back into the spotlight.

'Oh come on. Did I say a million? A hundred thousand? No – and a thousand pounds is nothing these days. Peanuts. I mean, remember "Blue Peter"? Look how much they managed to raise for starving kids in Africa. Two million. Think about it: two million quid. How many kids in this hall now watch "Blue Peter"?'

Three hands went up: Wendy Backbender, Betty Skinner and with great disdain, Ruthie. I sat on mine. He counted and shrugged.

'There you are. Look at that. Three out of seventy-five,' and his eyes rolled in his head like a fruit machine, as he calculated something. 'That's only four per cent. Blimey, if four per cent can raise two million then surely if all the kids in Swanswell pulled their weight they'd raise a thousand without even getting out of breath. So come on; am I right, or am I right?'

And he generously invited all the eager-beaver money-raisers to a grand meeting in Room Two during break. As the assembly squeezed itself out of the double doors after the first lesson bell, Stoney made a point of coming over to congratulate Chico.

'That was very impressive,' he noted and Chico smiled modestly. 'Very speedy calculating I must say. Perhaps I should've put you in 'O' level maths after all.'

'When you start studying the Maths of the Street,' Chico informed him coolly, 'I'll come and join you.'

Stoney snorted knowingly and left it at that. Then it was my turn to congratulate Chico in the corridor. He seemed very pleased with himself too. 'Any time old son – just say the word.'

And he waited for me to say the word. So then he made me an offer. 'I mean, if you want any help in raising the cash. Just say the word.'

'Right . . . er . . . fine,' I stumbled and stuttered. This was tricky. It wasn't that I was ungrateful; just embarrassed. Chico's problem was that he was Son of the original Cockney Wideboy: great to watch, great to listen to, always good for a laugh – from a safe distance. Close up you couldn't trust him a centimetre. Ever since he'd come to us all the way from London with his stepdad, he'd been trying to con us into or out of one thing or another. He just loved to part fools from their money.

'I mean, I have several excellent money-raising schemes lined up already,' he added, pulling a crumpled sheet out of his Harrington jacket pocket.

I glanced at my watch and at last he noticed that I wasn't too keen on his ideas any more. Sad really.

'We'll see how it goes . . .' I suggested and nodding he screwed up his bit of paper in front of me. So I left the whole thing in mid-air and hoped it would stay there.

Room Two was not exactly bursting with crowds of people that break. Ruthie and her gang had boycotted the meeting for some reason and so had Chico, which shows even he can take a hint. I worried about Ruthie though.

Anyway, it was now my turn to do the winding up.

First I passed round a piece of paper for a list of ideas.

After about ten minutes of shouting and laughing and pushing off chairs, the tattered, torn and scribbled sheet was picked up off the floor and handed to me by an apologetic Davy Cole.

Ignoring the rude drawing smack in the centre I looked at these wonderful ideas. Suddenly I felt very angry.

'Who put, "Go to Bristol and do mugging"?' I shouted. Three yobbos giggled as they put their hands up. 'Right! You lot can get out for a start.'

And they left. So did those who put 'Rob a post office', 'Steal Cars', 'Kidnap Thornie' and 'Sponsored Orgy'. Jammy swore he was serious when he put 'Busking in Berkeley', but I chucked him out all the same.

I sighed in despair as I looked round at the remainder. Davy Cole, my true and trusty friend, Beryl and Cheryl the twins; Bonehead Wilkins with his finger up to his knuckles in his nostril and Noddy Bright. The same faithful bunch of dimboes who'd signed on at the beginning. The Famous Five. All well-meaning kids who wouldn't even raise a laugh let alone a thousand pounds. Serves me right for spurning Chico. He may have been a crook but he knew how to get things going.

When I showed him the list of suggestions after break in Spanish, he didn't look very impressed. He rolled his eyes and calculated. 'Thirty quid for the sponsored event, maybe. 2p for the busking, 3p for this dog-jog rubbish, but a good two hundred for that Bring and Buy job, which if I remember, was how those Blue Peter wallies totted up their million . . . Muchas graçias niño. . . .'

He handed it back hastily as Rhys-Owen came over to investigate. We did some Spanish and waited for him to prowl elsewhere. After he'd gone, Chico flipped his book shut and leaned over. 'Look, Ducker, old muchacho; what you want is something original. Like a video nasty; now they're all the rage with kids round here . . . comprendido?'

'Madre de Dios, que loro!' I laughed at him. Video nasty? That showed even he could have daft ideas. The only way we could make a decent video nasty would be to film a Humanities lesson. But I could see what he meant. These days there were sponsored events all over the place.

Next tutor period Stoney kindly devoted all of it, all twenty minutes, to thinking up good, original events to sponsor. You can imagine his favourite, especially with a class like 3L.

A hand-picked bunch of kids: Chico, Maria Kelly, Davy, Gary, Rexy Trencher and me all lined up in front of the class clutching the little sponsor forms that Stoney had run off the Banda, personally. A sponsored silence! Stoney made a real meal of it. One by one he hung placards over our heads and told the grinning class: 'Now then you lot, until four o'clock, nobody, but nobody must address a single word to any one of these persons, nor let any one of these persons address a single word to anybody else.'

He lifted my placard and tapped it. 'This is why they are wearing little signs round their necks saying, "Sponsored Silence." From now on these people must not utter one word, or make any other sound. Got that, all of you?'

'Yes, sir . . . oops, sorry, sir!' blurted out Davy before disappearing under a hail of fists and elbows. For a moment Stoney looked as if he doubted the success of his master-plan.

'Hypnotise him. Lock him in the book-cupboard. Put him out on the field. Put him in Thornie's boot!' the rest of the class suggested while Davy went red with rage but kept the rude answers to himself.

We all thought that lessons would be easier if we weren't supposed to talk; especially drama. I mean what on earth can you do in a drama lesson if you can't talk? We had reckoned without Miss Silverberg.

You guessed it; she made us do mime. All six of us, still

with our placards on, had to mime something for the class. Gary did a weight lifter which came as no surprise; Rexy did Millwall fans booting heads in, which also came as no surprise. Chico did a brilliant magician, to our amazement, and I did a superb dolphin, only nobody had the brains to recognise it.

We had to keep it up even during the lunch hour. Imagine queuing up for lunch – sausage, chips and baked beans, followed by ice-cream and chocolate sauce – delicious – without saying a word. You had to point to the salt if you couldn't reach it and kids would go: 'Sorry, Ducker? D'you want something?' while putting the salt on the next table. 'Sorry, Ducker, can't quite hear you. You wanted the salt was it? Eh? Speak up then!'

Just as I was about to give a really sarcastic answer, Maria Kelly's knuckles bruised my arm. I went without salt. Bad for you anyway.

Room Two was like an exam room after lunch. We had to sit spread out, arms folded, not even allowed to listen to the radio. We just sat thinking of the eighty-five quid we were going to raise. A great start. But Old Stoney, the sadist, was loving it. Every now and then the door would open carefully and let in the noises of normal, day-to-day living and the occasional teacher. They'd just stand there, leering smugly at us and nod, or say something to Stoney like, 'What a brilliant idea,' or 'We ought to have these more often,' and Stoney would chortle into his beard and dare us even to think of an insult.

Thornie himself put in a guest appearance. He looked at each and every one of us, nodded in satisfaction, then turning to Stoney said, ever so wittily, 'What a brilliant idea,' and, 'We ought to do this more often'. Thornie laughed and Stoney heaved the slightest of sighs but still managed to chuckle cheerily. 'Yes indeed, Mr Thorne. Ha-ha!'

But the agony of it. It was so BORING!! After only six minutes I was squirming on my chair, like it was a hot plate, and I could see the others felt exactly the same.

It was soon over though. In fact, the ordeal was over a lot sooner than anyone had expected.

'What went wrong?' the rest of the class asked as Stoney ripped up our sponsor sheets into sixteenths and in a furious temper.

'Don't ask me; ask that animal over there with the blond curls,' I snarled bitterly, glaring at Davy who was in the corner, red as hot coal too.

'Ain't my fault,' he whined pathetically. 'How was I to know we'd have baked beans for lunch! Anyway; it was your lot's fault as well, for laughing. You made a bigger row than me.'

'Eighty-five quid that could have been!' I reminded him. Yes, it would have been the best possible start, but now – gone with the wind.

4. Marathon Men, and Women!

'Needs to discipline himself more and not encourage indiscipline among others' Drama, Miss Silverberg

Once again the whole thing was the joke of the school, which was a pity, as people had just started taking us seriously.

Thank goodness somebody with just the right flair and initiative came up with an interesting idea. Me. We needed something that was the same but different, right? So we'd have a massive canal marathon from Sharpness to Slimbridge, only instead of running it, we'd do it in special stages.

'Five-legged race, what the hell's that?' they all echoed my idea, frowning.

'Four blokes, er . . . or girls of course, with their legs tied together.'

They all tapped their temples and screwed their fingers.

'Half-a-mile Piggy Back? D'you know how far half a mile is?' shouted Gary. 'You couldn't even walk it, Ducker.'

'Half-a-mile chariot race?' droned Bonehead. 'What's that then?' I ignored him.

'Half-a-mile Leap-Frog?' shrieked Maria Kelly. 'That's bad enough for the frogs but what about the kids underneath?'

'We take it in turns,' I shouted dangerously at her, then, trying to push back the invisible walls of panic and protest, continued: 'We want to attract people's attention, right? To get money out of them, right? So we give them something funny and exciting to watch. . . .'

'Yeah – *you* doing five-legged races, chariot-races and leap-frogging, all on your own,' Killer Maria retorted.

But in the end, and as usual it was a very noisy, long-drawn out end, they decided to go through with it. No less than sixty kids volunteered, mostly third years, all in Swanswell tee-shirts: they'd had them printed years ago and they were still trying to get rid of them. The art department, that is Sandy Sanderson, had made up a huge banner, ten feet wide on poles, saying 'Swanswell Swimming-Pool Appeal', in blue and green letters.

As the great day got nearer and I was starting to feel quite chuffed about my achievement, everybody started to feel more and more excited. Would we be on telly? In the papers? Would they all get good reports?

In a way it was funny who joined in and who didn't. Yobs like Barnsie, Burroughs and Cox from 3F were dead keen, whereas Ruth hadn't shown the slightest bit of interest in the whole enterprise. I thought it was because of the row we'd had after my report.

But, that evening, I bumped into her in the market square. I'd just come out of Streeter's laden with chews and reading a comic when she stalked out of the bakers at the same time. I hurriedly stuffed the comic under my Harrington and unwrapped a bubbly.

'Honestly, Ducker!' she moaned over her cottage loaf. 'I don't believe it. You still read comics!'

'I do not,' I muttered and bent down to pick it up off the pavement. I straightened out the crumpled front page and tried not to look guilty. 'I don't read them. I, er . . . look at the drawings. The artwork's brilliant, and you know I'm good at art, Ruthie.'

'Ducker, you're not good at anything, especially lying,' she snapped. 'And don't call me Ruthie.'

She turned on her heel and marched off round the corner into the High Street, knowing I'd follow. Suddenly she gave a shriek and jumped back. An electric wheelchair came burning rubber round the corner, two wheels off the ground, and then headed straight for me, tooting its horn merrily.

It was old Mr Pegson out to get some more horse manure tobacco from Streeter's. He grinned behind his whiskery, white moustache, cheeks as red as berries, spectacles glinting like kamikaze goggles, and missed me by centimetres. It may have been a rickety old machine but at close range it was still lethal. He waved at me, lifted his tweed hat to Ruthie and screeched a sharp bend into Streeter's where there were more shouts and screams and crashing noises.

'That was close,' I gasped at Ruthie who was still pale. 'Are you OK Ruth?'

'Course I am,' she replied, angry at her own faint-heartedness, but let me carry the bread. This gave me the chance we'd both been waiting for to ask her why she wasn't helping with the Swimming Pool Appeal.

'Look, I don't mind raising money if it's for a worthy cause,' she explained as we waited to cross the road. 'But frankly I don't consider a swimming pool to be a good cause. And I don't like the people running it either. Trust you to recruit Chico Marks instead of the obvious man for the job, Des Grisewald.

'Chico isn't flipping running it, thank you very much,' I snapped back, feeling my blood simmer at the mention of Grisewald.

'You know what I think of Super-creep. I wouldn't ask his help if both my arms dropped off. I'm doing it on my own, all on my own for a change, and all you can do –'

'Look what Chico Marks said about "Blue Peter",' she interrupted. 'They raised two million pounds. Yes, but what for? For millions of starving kids, not for a place to swim when it's hot. You know as well as I do that there are loads of worthy causes round here that could do with the money. Old people. I mean look at Mr Pegson. He could do with a new wheelchair for a start.'

'Blimey,' I muttered, hearing the wasp-like buzz of his mean machine in the distance. 'What's wrong with the one he drives like a maniac now? It only goes forty miles an hour, I suppose.'

She folded her arms and have me a heavy, sarcastic sigh. 'It keeps breaking down and he wants one that goes up kerbs,' she informed me, gripping my arms and smiling sweetly as he zoomed past us down the road, scattering pedestrians, dogs and dustbins. 'They cost nearly a thousand pounds, too.'

'Ruth darling,' I told her straight, 'Swanswell raised its share of money for starving kids at Christmas, remember? And besides, there isn't enough money in the world to help all the charities going round. I want to raise money for the pool because . . . I want to, I do think it's a great idea and you're being your usual toffee-nosed vicar's daughter self by not joining in with the rest of us.'

And with that I turned smartly and quickly on my heel.

I didn't see her by the canal on Saturday either. I wasn't surprised, just disappointed for some reason. She might have been hiding in the crowds I suppose. Yes, crowds; they'd turned up in crowds to see the great Swanswell Canal Marathon. And the press was there, too. One reporter and one photographer from the *Gazette*.

'So it's only five miles then,' he said, sounding disappointed after we'd posed proudly under Sandy's blue and green banner.

'Yes, but look at all the different ways of doing it,' I pointed out, trying to look over his notebook to see what he'd put. He still didn't sound very impressed. He was glancing round over my head as if something really interesting was bound to be happening – somewhere else. Then his face lit up with an idea.

'So . . . it's really competitive? Groups, teams of four racing against each other along the canal? Girls too?' I nodded. He scribbled. 'All for a ten quid prize? Not much is it? But now then. Could it be in any way, you know, dodgy? Risky? Dangerous even?'

'Dangerous?' I repeated carefully, wondering what he was after.

'Dangerous? Not 'alf mate!' chirped a Cockney accent and Chico stepped in to add a bit of excitement to the Gazette's report. He'd only come to watch the fun, not to compete of course. At least he wasn't still offended by my little snub earlier in the week.

'Dangerous?' he repeated, coughing out a laugh. *Gazette*-man scribbled. 'Six kids got hurt yesterday in the practice alone.'

G-man paused, looked up. 'Is that with an S?'

'Eh? No it was the chariot race. That's a real killer. And of course they'll be really tired after that. So when they come staggering along to do Piggy-back and Leap-frog – it'll be slaughter. They'll be dropping like flies. Falling in the canal, too, I shouldn't wonder.'

'Fantastic,' G-man repeated. 'Fan-tastic. Now then, er . . . kid; where's the best place for a . . . you know . . . a good picture?'

'Chariot race, definitely. By the first lock gate.'

Next he asked us which one of the haggard, greying, paunchy men in Swanswell tee-shirts was the headmaster.

'What was all that in aid of?' I asked Chico as G-man practically sprinted over to Thornie who, or course, was the most haggard-looking of all that day.

'Publicity, Ducker,' Chico chirped back with a nudge. I made a point of walking past Thornie's interview on my way to the start, just as G-man was asking.

'Mister Thorne, what do the parents think about their children, some of whom are only young girls, being put through a series of arduous and potentially dangerous physical ordeals just to raise money for a swimming pool. . . ?'

I saw Thornie's eyes narrow and he spluttered. 'I-I don't quite understand the phrasing of that question. . . .'

Still, it was Thornie, who, breaking free from the grip of the press, took up the starter's gun and waited for us all to huddle under the banner before pulling the trigger. With a crack, a volley of camera-clicks and hearty cheers all round, the teams were hobbling off in the first stage.

The first stage, the five-legged race, was supposed to be the easiest. The 'A' team: me, Gary, Davy and Rexy Trencher had been practising like mad all week because we knew from the start what the different stages were going to be like. Others may have found the chariot race difficult, but for the 'A' team the five-legged race was the big problem. Other groups had one left foot at one end but we had two left feet in the middle and Davy Cole owned both of them. He just couldn't get himself synchronised with the rest of us. Apart from that, once we fell over we lay like a beetle on its back, kicking its legs in the air and finding it very difficult to get back up.

We were about tenth by the end of the first stage until Braddock, the sports teacher, put us out of our misery and called out through his megaphone, 'Right lads – change – chariot race!'

We soon started overtaking the others who were falling over, collapsing or just crawling along very slowly. We actually moved into second place and then it happened.

Rexy let out a shriek and fell over, pulling me off Gary's back with him. As we collapsed in a heap, Pittbrook Pirates, who were in third place, guffawed gleefully and thundered past.

'Sorry lads, I been bloody stung,' Rexy moaned searching his leg for the tell-tale swelling. He couldn't find it, but

I saw a movement in the bushes by the path and heard this deep chuckle that almost sounded like Barnsie's eldest brother. Barnsie junior was skipper of the Pirates.

By the time we changed to Piggy-back, we were actually in the lead with no one there to beat us and me wondering why Chico had said that Pittbrook Pirates were hot favourites. But suddenly Davy shouted across to Gary something about a rope. Gary kept plodding on and so did Rexy, until there we were again doing our centipede act, lying on the floor all eight legs in the air and four-letter words.

As I stood up slowly waiting for my 'horse' to do the same, I heard that deep laugh coming from behind another bush. Just as I was considering shooting Davy to put him out of his misery who should come trampling past us to take over the lead but the Pirates: Barnsie, Clark, Burroughs and Cox.

'Oh dear,' sang Barnes happily. 'How careless of my brother to leave that rope lying about like that – cheerio, suckers!'

So that was what had happened. I saw then that the rope was tied to a stake by the bank and led to that bush. The instant we'd stepped over it someone had pulled it straight and sent us flying.

As Nico Barnes lumbered out of hiding to retrieve his rope, Davy leapt to his feet in one jump and raced after Nico's smaller brother, leader of the Pittbrook Pirates.

'Come on lads, this is war!'

'But what about Piggyback?' I shouted after the three of them as they sought revenge.

'Stuff your Piggyback, Ducker and get stuck in!' answered Gary.

And before I could stop them, they'd tripped up the Pirates who were now kicking *their* legs in the air. Horses and riders struggled to their feet in time to get their heads cracked together by Gary and a chance to try out another of Davy's swimming courses. And soon they were all in the canal paddling about quite successfully with Davy brushing his hands at the edge very proudly.

'Right, you lot!' roared Bradley, the deputy Head, clutching his clip-board and rushing towards us. 'You're all disqualified and I'll see you in my office on Monday morning.'

'But sir, they tried to nobble us,' Davy protested and Bradley did actually notice Barnsie the elder stalking by the bushes. He'd come back to rescue his little brother and was holding his rope and air-rifle.

Other teams were staggering past us, and spectators too, cheering them on. The *Gazette* team had arrived as well though they seemed more interested in the canal itself than the Marathon.

The final event was the Leap-frog and right from the back a team of girls, 'Kelly's Heroes', overtook the leading half a dozen boys and won the Marathon by a length: Maria Kelly, her sister Bernadette, and two other fourth year girls. That's what I call adding insult to injury.

5. Minor Reprimands, but Major Rivals

'He has shown an abundance of energy and enthusiasm this term, for doing the wrong thing at the wrong time' Mr M. J. Stone, Tutor

Monday was almost a time of triumph and rejoicing. We had raised three hundred and sixty pounds and that was nearly half way there. But we also had a quick session being shouted at in Bradley's wind-tunnel.

'Pity about the photo,' Thornie noted ruefully in his office, taking his turn that break. On page two was a large picture of the Pittbrook Pirates in the canal, with Davy standing at the edge of the bank, pointing and laughing. People could read the caption and make up their own minds. 'Boys from Swanswell cooling off in the canal during their Grand Marathon.' The bit about parents and arduous ordeals was confined to the last paragraph but one, and Thornie got his own back by saying nasty things about the government and cuts in education expenditure for three long paragraphs before that.

'Good to see youngsters using initiative constructively,' he quoted himself and tapped the paragraph meaningfully. 'When I said that I did not mean pushing each other in the canal or having punch-ups on the bank.'

He put the paper down and paused dramatically without taking his eyes off us. 'I could do with a thousand pounds. The pool is a good idea – thank you, Ducker. Now, I appreciate you four were provoked, but I would rather not have any trouble, especially as your Grand Appeal has started to attract the attention of the gutter press. And if you think about it, gentlemen, raising a thousand pounds over a heap of dead bodies and amid the smouldering ruins of the school will not be such a great achievement. Not that I would ever let you get as far as that. You do understand my concern in this matter. Now the next time I want to see you is clutching a large bag of money. Got it?'

'We got it, you ungrateful old bastard,' muttered Davy, seconds after Thornie had kicked us out.

Back in Room Two the celebrations were continuing. With three hundred and fifty quid under our belts, that is once they'd collected it off the sponsors, there was an upsurge of new-found confidence and more and more people wanted to get involved, offering their ideas: most of them ridiculous or suicidal. Just like the saying goes: 'Nothing succeeds like success'. However, trouble was on its way.

I had just turned to Chico to say, 'Oh yeah, and thanks for your wonderful publicity. Thornie's just been biting our heads off with gratitude.' And Chico had just replied, 'Ducker, old mate, there is no such thing as bad publicity,' when the first of our enemies struck.

Room Two was almost empty, with the rest of the class already beginning the long trek to science. Gary, Davy and I were sorting out suggestions. Chico was hiding from winners.

'Ooh look, it's the 'A' team,' sang a voice sarcastically from the doorway. It was Ruth Goody Two-Shoes, Dawn Devonshire and Wendy Backbender, an enormous girl who stood behind them, over them and blocked out the light from the corridor.

They walked jauntily in and Dawn went up to Gary. 'Hi Hunky! How's Gary Steroid this macho morning?' she said and flicked his crucifix. Ruth sat on the table and smiled sexily, as sexily as she could.

'Come on Gar', pump up some of those muscles for us.'

'Yeah, right, which ones,' he grunted huskily and started to turn himself into a trophy, till I tapped his forearm and shook my head.

'Anyway Supersteroid, you shouldn't wear one of these unless you believe,' and sounding like her real self Ruth tapped the silver crucifix against his heaving, buckling chest.

'All right you lot,' shouted Davy angrily, 'what d'you want?'

'A challenge,' she stated coldly. 'A little challenge for money-grubbing Ducker and the greedy rest of you. If you've got the guts that is. . . .'

'And the challenge is?' I jeered uneasily. The bell jangled and the rumpus of Lesson Exodus began to rumble through the corridor. Wendy flicked the door shut with her thumb and forefinger.

'So you've raised three hundred and fifty pounds,' Ruth said with arms folded. 'Well, I'll tell you something else. I reckon Ducker's got some pretty unhealthy ideas about the world, and if he thinks there isn't enough money to help all the charities in the world therefore we should all stop caring for people, I think he should be taught a lesson and be cured of this – for his own good of course.'

'I never said anything of the sort,' I spluttered. She was beginning to tremble, which meant she was getting really angry at something.

'We're going to race you, Ducker,' she told me, controlling herself.

'Race us?' laughed Supersteroid.

'Yes, race you to the top. We are also going to raise a thousand pounds,' explained the gorgeous Dawn. 'But here's the challenge. Whoever reaches one thousand pounds first, or makes the most by the end of term, wins the Grand Prize.'

'Oh yeah, and what sort of fantastic prize do we win?' asked Davy.

'More of a forfeit really,' Wendy put in with a deep voice. 'We win whatever you've raised for us.'

'So if you've raised a thousand and we've raised nine hundred,' I asked, sounding like a loser already, 'we forfeit ours and you collect nineteen hundred?'

'What a load of rubbish!' sneered Davy as the girls nodded at me.

'And anyway, that ain't fair. . . .'

'For God's sake, Ruth,' I shouted, angry myself now, 'what have you got against us? This is really stupid.'

'For one thing, it shouldn't be parents who have to fork out for your little pool, you ought to ask the government or somebody. Anyway, are you lot chickening out already? I am disappointed. . . .'

We lads stood shoulder to shoulder and bleated 'No', but didn't sound too confident about it.

'Right – we're starting on Saturday with a sponsored disco.'

'How original!' laughed Gary scornfully as Ruthie dipped into her bag.

'Twenty-four-hour disco. Here, you can sponsor us.' And they handed over sheets of paper that were crammed with scribbly signatures. We did not add ours.

'Relax, you blokes,' soothed Chico after the girls marched off to science. He'd been watching all this with a mixture of fascination and amusement. 'It's as good as in the bag. You're nearly half way there already. And when you win their loot you can add that to your expenses.'

'Expenses?' I queried.

He blushed slightly. 'Well yeah, now that it's suddenly for real you'll need all sorts of extra ideas, but good ones this time.'

He stood there as we queued up in the gloom waiting for me to ask him what a good idea was and I waited for him to wander off. He'd spent all break on the run from kids who'd backed Kelly's Heroes and wanted their winnings. He'd got out of it by giving them their money back claiming all bets were off because of nobbling. He'd put all his money on Pittbrook Pirates of course.

And then who should come to us outside Room Twenty-four but the Burroughs gang: Clark, Denny and Spencer.

'Heard you raised three hundred quid,' Clark growled, drooling at the thought of all that loot.

'Yeah and it's locked in the school safe where your thieving hands can't touch it,' Davy told them toughly.

'We only come to offer our help,' added Spencer Burroughs in an injured tone of voice. That was like the Mafia offering to guard the Pope.

'We do fancy a sponsored bike ride round Britain, that 'ud raise more 'an a thousand pounds, we do reckon.'

'But you Burroughs kids ain't got a bike,' Davy pointed out. They looked at each other and sort of tensed.

'Well, no – we'd buy it from the money you'd lend us out of the funds raised so far.'

'You mean put it on expenses?' I clarified for them. They all beamed at me bright-eyed and bushy-tailed.

'Cheerio,' growled Gary and started to push them towards the stairs.

'Listen you big 'eads,' they hissed at us. 'You'd rather have us with you than against you, eh?'

I waved them good-bye, unimpressed by their threats. 'OK, Ducker,' snarled Clark. 'You asked for it – you'd better watch out from now on, you . . . aaaagh!'

Davy told them to vacate the premises and leaving the Burroughs gang tumbling down the stairs, we trooped into the evil-smelling lab. They must have overheard what Chico was saying.

But there was no doubt about it – we were in trouble. Those girls were much better at raising money than we were; they'd proved that last Christmas. As for the Burroughs gang, I wondered if we ought to get the money we'd raised transferred to Fort Knox.

If Ruthie was unimpressed by our achievement, my old man was even less impressed. When I got home that afternoon he beckoned me into the bar with a rolled up newspaper. The bar was where we had our man-to-man chats: after every report and parents' evening.

He tapped me on the head with his paper truncheon and told me to sit. I glanced at my watch openly and tried to look bored out of my skull. He opened up his paper and re-read the article on page two.

'Look,' he sighed and put the paper down. It unrolled itself with a flick, like a trap opening. 'Is all this really a good idea? I mean, I know you're trying very hard to get back into the school's good books; but with this? Raising money? Who d'you think you are, Bob Gelding. . . ?'

'Geldof!' I moaned loudly. He paused, purple. 'You mean Bob Geldof, *Sir* Bob Geldof.'

'I know what I mean,' he thundered. 'I mean I don't want a son who's good at raising money – I want a son who's good at school, who comes out at the end with a fistful of 'O' levels and 'A' levels. That's what I want. And I don't see how you can do both. . . .'

'But I am good at school – now,' I groaned in protest. 'You wait till you see my report sheet. Every day I give it to Stoney and every day he ticks it and gives me a pat on the head. I got four goods today. . . .'

'Oh yes, a marvellous effort I must say,' he burbled purply. 'Let me see, how long has this been going on, why it must be almost a week, yes? Splendid stuff. But let me tell you something I think you ought to know. . . .'

He paused. I shifted uncomfortably. It sounded very ominous. 'When I was at that wretched third year parents' evening I practically had to beg on bended knees for you to do the 'O' level courses – all eight of them. As far as they were concerned you were classic CSE material. And I almost had to get down on my hands and knees before each,

49

separate Head of Department to convince them otherwise. . . .'

He took a deep breath. 'I did not like doing it. Now bear that in mind. I've already had to look a fool once on your behalf.'

I suddenly felt really embarrassed. Stoney had told me something similar but only as a bluff and a threat. Fancy Dad falling for it. Now that he'd got his breath and pride back he continued.

'If there is the slightest hint of trouble arising from this stupid money-raising business, or the faintest sign of your work suffering, the whole thing's off and you, my boy, go under curfew.'

He glanced over his shoulder towards the kitchen and shuddered. 'Good job your mother hates newspapers.'

'But I wasn't even involved in that punch-up,' I told him eagerly.

'Oh, so there was a punch-up. I thought as much,' he concluded triumphantly. Then he rolled up his truncheon again and got to his feet. 'You have been warned.'

And he shuffled back into the kitchen to show immediate interest in one of my mother's latest poems.

6. Cricket the Money-spinner?

'He represented the school well in the cricket team. I wish him the best of luck in the County Trials'
P.E., Mr Braddock

Whatever else happened today, nothing could spoil it. We had cricket after school: a return match with this poncy comprehensive from Thornbury. Strangely enough, the estate they came from was quite posh. Neatly-cut lawns and cherry trees all over the place. A dormitory town my dad called it. The grown-ups worked and played in Bristol and left the streets free for the kids to stroll around twelve hours a day. It sounded like paradise, almost. All the freedom you needed to bore yourself silly. They'd been lucky in April beating us by eight wickets. Revenge would soon be ours. As you may have guessed I don't like cricket, I love it.

Mind you the day didn't get off to the best possible start. After a minor setback and a major triumph everything had suddenly begun to go wrong. We'd run into opposition and run out of ideas at the same time. Some wanted to do sponsored headstands, human pyramids and rubbish like that. And every five minutes Chico would breeze up to me saying, 'Call that a good idea?' and wait for me to ask his expert, highly illegal advice. Worse than that, rumour had it that the girls were getting a lot of help from Supercreep himself, Des Grisewald, the Youth leader.

Des was in the Art room that break, as usual, pretending to meet his fellow Commie, Sandy Sanderson the art master, but really chatting up yet another Sixth-former. Des was the idol of all the girls: good, bad or ugly. He spoke like a second-rate DJ, wore a crucifix and went to church, sometimes, and so had Ruthie Pendryll eating out of his hand. He also smoked and swore politely when he played football.

'Hey, Des, what's the idea of helping the girls against us?' Gary asked as we cornered him by the mezzanine steps. 'That ain't fair.'

He raised his arm and smiled. 'Come on fellas, cool it,' he oozed. 'Don't you realise how up-tight the girls were after Ducker's wisecracks to Ruth?' And with a glint of his dung-brown eyes he shifted the blame on to me. 'Once they make up their minds about something, they just get, you know, terrifically committed with the whole jazz. So now they're really into raising a cool thou'! You know what girls are like. . . .'

'Not as well as you do,' I muttered loudly, looking at Dinah Spargo, who was very annoyed at us for interrupting her adulation.

'But we're really into raising a cool thou' as well,' Gary told him.

'Look fellas, just stay cool,' he beamed, squirming past us. 'Just, you know, carry on making money and I . . . I'll see what I can do . . . OK?'

And he carried on chatting up Dinah, who was a right weirdo, I must say. She wanted to be an art student, and dyed her hair pink and white and had it all brushed up, wore purple eye-shadow and despite the school rule about jewellery, large brass earings – straight from her granny's curtain rails no doubt.

'Lads, lads, don't be down-hearted,' chirped a cockney accent behind us. 'OK, so you saw the names on their sponsor sheets and they may clean up a hundred quid between them. But now's the time to get your little show back on the road.'

'By doing what?' I asked him out of desperation. Chico

opened his mouth as if to suggest something really out-
rageous, thought better of it and chose a couple of safer
ones. As we strolled from Art room to Youth Centre, I
fancied his idea of a bring and buy sale. As for his Video
Nasty he had to be joking and I couldn't understand why
he persisted.

'Bring-and-buy sales, though dead boring, are reliable
money-spinners, Ducker old muchacho,' he said, really
pleased that at last I had let him become our road manager.
He glanced at his watch, muttered, 'Time for a quickie,'
and raced off to the science labs so that we arrived leaderless at the leaderless Youth Centre.

As I watched Gary practising his side spin on the snooker
table, I wondered how the girls got all those signatures so
quickly in the first place. Wendy Backbender on the disco
floor was like an iceberg on the Severn; Ruthie didn't
exactly dance, but vibrated sedately, while Dawn Devonshire leaned against the wall repeating 'No thanks' to one
bloke after another.

Could things get worse? On the way to lessons I strolled
past the notice board and sensed something was wrong. I
looked at the team notice and saw that Murphy's name was
crossed out.

'He has to go to the dentist after school, he says,' muttered
Gary over my shoulder. That was all we needed. Murph
was our fastest bowler and second-best batsman. What a
time to have his molars molested.

'I hope they pull a few out,' I muttered bitterly.

'Yeah, front ones too,' Gary agreed.

'Without anaesthetic,' I concluded as Thornie came
storming down the corridor sweeping up the stragglers. His
manner changed when he saw what we were looking at.

'You will win tonight, I hope,' he enquired anxiously. He
and the Head of Thornbury Green hated each other by all
accounts.

'Have no fear, sir,' I quipped confidently. 'Ducker the Destroyer will win the day. . . .'

'Will he?' Thornie grunted, decidedly unimpressed. 'As destruction seems to be one of his great skills these days I'm relieved to see it put to good use for a change.'

He pointed over my head down the corridor. I chuckled politely and then asked him the question I'd been waiting patiently with.

'About the pool, sir.' That magic word held him spellbound. 'Couldn't the, er . . . government pay some money towards it?' I asked tentatively.

He nearly fell about in convulsions of laughter. When he finally controlled himself he looked at me watery-eyed. 'The government give us money? This government? Where on earth d'you think we are – the Falklands?'

And that was it. He didn't detect my note of despair or reluctance to continue with the enterprise that was beginning to drive me mad. Davy sat next to me in Humanities and copied my worksheet.

'What d'you think, Ducker? Braddock asked me to play in the cricket team,' he complained. Asking Davy to play was scraping the ground beneath the barrel.

'I hope you said "No,"' I answered. Fortunately he had. 'If we lose against Thornbury I'll eat the stumps,' I hissed.

'That's what it looks like,' Davy speculated gloomily.

Not every speculator was gloomy about it though.

'Look lads,' said Chico, who was the second worst cricketer in the school, 'here is a golden opportunity to raise a few quid. Do not let it slip past. . . .'

This pep talk came during lunch. We had curry that smelt and tasted of armpit. As I shovelled soggy rice on to my bent fork I wondered how you could raise money from a cricket match. How else?

'A book?' I squawked distastefully. 'After the mess you

made of that marathon? If you let people bet on the winners, who the hell is going to bet on us?'

'Well, I might, for a start,' he said. I shook my head.

'And if Thornie ever finds out he'll have you for middle stump. You know what he thinks about gambling. . . .'

'It rots the soul,' Chico intoned dolefully then giggled. 'Ducker, the reason why you will never raise a lot of money, or grow to a ripe old age is because you worry too much. Now leave it all to Uncle Chico.'

And with a pat on my whitening cheeks he left it at that. I suppose his confidence could have been inspired by the fact that I was captain. You see, despite being lazy and getting in and out of trouble and lousy reports, I happened to be the best swing bowler Swanswell had ever seen. I was so good I didn't even need to be modest about it.

Bowling swing was easy at Swanswell, I believed. I had this theory about the damp atmosphere helping the ball move in the air. It certainly paid off when we played at home, especially evening matches.

'By the way, lads,' Chico poked his head round the door and told us as we got ready in the changing rooms, 'I do not wish to demoralise you, but Thornbury are 20–1 on. No one seems to favour your chances, except me of course.'

The team looked hard at him, then at me for some reason. I took him to one side, into the showers in fact. 'You have considered the possibility that if we lose you will have to pay out a small fortune?'

He thought about it, then nodded. 'So you need an awful lot of money? Where's it going to come from, Chico?'

I suddenly knew the answer the instant I asked the question. 'Expenses,' he stated economically. Then once again the chummy pat on the chalky cheeks. 'Come on skipper, have some faith in yourself. We shall not lose.'

Thornbury turned up late. We were already out on the pitch practising when they turned up in their mini-coach, along with their fans, who arrived noisily on scooters.

The scooter gang: dozens of them, aged between fourteen and seventeen, would come buzzing up the A38 at weekends and holidays and cruise round the villages annoying us, or fill up Arnold's Grill in Berkeley. So far they'd never stayed around long enough for real trouble. But there they were that evening, all piling to the field; fifth and sixth-formers, former pupils of Thornbury High and their teeny-bopper pillions eagerly awaiting their captain to lead his unbeaten team on to the grass. As I cut a practice catch to Gary, I could see Chico moving among them with his little book.

But as far as I was concerned, the worst thing about Thornbury was their captain, known to us as Flash Gordon. Tall and skinny, he had short blond, spiky hair, wore Madness tee-shirts and an earring. He fancied himself as God's gift to the willow and leather, and was all mouth and flannels. He batted, bowled, made acrobatic catches and appealed for everything.

We lost the toss, which wasn't the best of omens, and he put us in to bat. Almost immediately he was doing his appeal-for-everything act.

'OWIZZEE! Come on umpire! Get him off!' He leapt up like an albino Maori doing a war-dance.

'All right, all right,' snapped Stoney, who was umpire with one of their teachers. 'This isn't "Match of the Day"!'

'No,' said Flash in a loud voice as he turned away, one hand still raised, 'and you're not Jimmy flipping Hill either. . . .'

If he'd been at Swanswell, Stoney would have inserted a stump up each nostril. But as he was a visitor Stoney gritted his teeth and ignored him.

Things had started badly. Their bowlers were fast and

furious, but a bit off the mark. Gary was clobbering them happily all over the pitch until Flash bowled him a bouncer and he skied it. He was caught for nineteen. I could have killed Stoney for giving me out lbw when I was on twenty-eight and the ball would have missed leg-stump by miles. After twenty overs we had made eighty-four. Flash Gordon's war-dance was getting more and more frenzied.

When it was their turn to bat they did not seem very impressed and were crashing us about all over the place. The scooter gang had started up this rhythmic accompaniment with rattling coke-cans. It was quite a good crowd too, which was good news for Chico. I noticed Thornie standing at the back, keeping a watchful eye on spectators and occasionally wincing at the cricket.

Then at fifty for two our luck seemed to change. I put myself on, after our fast bowlers had completely failed to soften them up and soon had the ball swinging through the air like a boomerang. They obviously hadn't seen anything like it. It was getting quite damp, too, despite the evening sun. Swallows were flying really low, hissing over the field, skimming the grass with their white bellies. The perfect atmosphere for Ducker the destroyer.

I did too. The only one who was being a bit awkward was Flash himself. He was trying to hit me across the Cotswolds, even coming down the wicket at me. In the end he closed his eyes, took a wild swinging swipe and fell back on to his stumps. Insult to injury. Lovely. Though how you can expect to hit a ball with your eyes closed beats me.

We won by fourteen runs and I took six for twenty-five! Didn't I tell you I was sensational? Chico took twenty-five quid and the less said about that the better. He was about to start boasting about his achievement in the changing room, but I bundled him out just as Stoney came strolling in with a very cheerful Thornie. They were discussing leg cutters of course. Thornie gave me a pat on the head.

As for the gallant opposition, they were the worst kind of losers: they complained about the light, the pitch, the umpires, even the spectators.

'You haven't heard the last of this, you two-faced swede bashers!' Flash called after me in the car park before he got into the mini-bus. The scooter escort had left a long time ago.

Chico caught up with me as I wandered across the car park to the pub. Somehow his congratulations didn't quite sound genuine. In the pub garden, however, he passed me his little tin. Then he produced a mirror. 'Oh dear, I forgot to give this back to Killer Maria,' he remembered, then waited. I was supposed to say 'Why'. She wanted the mirror for slapping on war-paint. He'd used it for squeezing little fat blackheads out of his nose. So?

'What did you want with Maria Kelly's mirror?' I asked.

'Eh? Oh . . . er . . . yes . . . well, I had something in my eyes,' he explained, trying to keep a straight face. 'God knows what it was. In there for ages. I was out on the field all through the game trying to find it. Hope I didn't distract any of the players, though it is possible I might have reflected the sun into their eyes, especially the good Thornbury batsmen. . . .'

A crack opened up in the garden lawn and seemed to swallow me up. 'You mean, you distracted the Thornbury batsmen by shining the mirror in their eyes?' I repeated with a dry throat. No wonder they weren't happy about losing. The bet was bad enough; this was risking fire from Heaven.

'This isn't cricket, Chico,' I moaned emptily. 'And you'll never get away with it. I knew I shouldn't have listened to you. . . .'

'But I did get away with it,' he yelped at me. 'And don't get all grumpy 'cos you thought Ducker the Destroyer had won the game all on his own. I didn't have to do it all that often anyway. You took two wickets all by yourself. Don't be so fussy. You're the cricketing hero of Swanswell and you made twenty-five quid, right? What's the problem?'

My problem was knowing where to start, there were so many problems, thanks to him. I stood there with my hands on hips.

'Look, Chico,' I began, feeling like Ruthie all of a sudden, 'if we can't get that money fair and square and trouble-free, we may as well not bother.'

'Tell that to the girls,' he replied. 'They'll know what to do with twenty-five quid, or do I mean three hundred and seventy five quid? Your total added to theirs when they win the race. Get it? But have it your own way. Be an honourable loser for all I care.'

He got up as well, but I grabbed the tin and held on to it. This time it was his turn to put hands on hips.

'Ducker, nobody makes money fair and square these days. The whole world's on the make. Fancy being in school for eight years and not learning that lesson yet.'

I didn't listen and he left me in a huff. I sat down slowly and thought things over. I sat there at the white metal table while gnats buzzed round my ears. The gaudy, torn umbrella was still up even though the sun was setting. I put the tin in my Gola bag. Should I give it back? Most of it was Thornbury money anyway, and they could afford it. Should I donate it anonymously to Ruthie's charity appeal? Not if it meant helping them to beat us. What a life! Problems after problems; pressure upon pressure. Even cricket wasn't safe these days.

7. Ruthie's Super-Disco and How I Saved the Day

> *'When inspired can produce highly imaginative and sensitive writing. However, inspiration has not visited him very often this term'* English, Mrs S. Potter

I felt really bad about Chico. He obviously thought he was doing me a favour and just could not get it into his crooked skull that as far as the Swanswell Appeal was concerned, the best favour he could do me was by not doing me any favours.

Some kids had branched out on their own and tried really hard to raise the totaliser mark that Sandy had fixed up in the foyer. It looked like a giant thermometer, with green mercury instead of red.

'Aren't you going to move it up twenty-five places?' a cockney voice whined in my ear and he stretched his arm out to oblige. I muttered 'later' and left it at that.

Noddy Bright was trying so hard it brought tears to the eyes – tears of laughter and embarrassment. Every other morning he'd come through the door of Room Two beaming all over his thick face and carrying a suitcase that rattled with junk and rubbish.

'There,' he would announce proudly, 'I found that lot in Gilpin's farmyard,' or, 'I got that load by the shore, you know where they had that battle years ago. . . .'

To which someone with more sense and better eye-sight would reply, 'Yeah, but that's a bottle-top, isn't it?' and flick the rusty brown treasure back at him. That morning we all gazed wearily once again at Noddy's proud display of treasures. Somehow seeing his standing there made me feel worse than Chico with his assistance.

'Here, what about that, then? A Roman sword, I reckon – or somebody's,' he declared confidently holding up a rusted mud-guard. 'You know old Gilpin's farm is ages old.' Then some old coins: doubloons from the sixties, and a golden half-penny from nineteen forty-seven. He had the nerve to look round eagerly like he was waiting for someone to say it was worth a fortune and raise him shoulder-high. Suddenly Gary lifted up a stick-like object.

'Isn't that a sword hilt?' he asked holding it up to the light.

'Don't you start,' I snapped; then explained with some expertise. 'That is a flipping Anglo-Saxon bottle-opener with the top rusted away. . . .'

Stoney wasn't too impressed either. He stormed in like a Viking invasion, bellowed, 'Get that rubbish off my desk,' and Noddy's treasure vanished back into obscurity with a cheap click of his imitation leather suitcase.

Thornie, as you might expect, wasn't too keen about the girls' threat to his pet project and he intervened personally. He didn't allow them to do a twenty-four hour disco; he insisted it be cut back to eighteen hours instead.

I wondered if it was worth telling people to ask for their sponsor-money back. After all, eighteen hours isn't half as impressive. I mean anybody can do that. Some of the girls do it seven days a week in the holidays, with the radio on all day, if you know what I mean.

However, at nine o'clock on the morning of Ruthie's Super-Disco, there I was having a sniff round. Des Super-creep had been there since six o'clock to ogle as much talent as he could. To my surprise there were quite a few people there. A banner hung over the entrance to the dining room, 'Swanswell Disco Marathon'. A couple of mums and dads, a young bloke in denims, who must have been a mate of Des's, all stood watching the dancers: mostly first years, but all of them girls. I don't know about you but first-year disco dancers make me laugh. Their faces tell you they think they're it and their puny bodies move like puppets on string.

I noticed Des Grisewald's mate start moving around among the crumpet, wandering from group to group carrying a large box-like bag. When I got closer I saw that his tee-shirt said 'Radio Severnside: The Best in News and Music!' News? What news? I had to listen in on this. 'How old are you, love? How old's your daughter? How long has she been doing it for? How much money has she raised so far? Fantastic!'

Fantastic? No wonder no one ever listened to Radio Severnside. And then he went up to Ruthie, stuffed the microphone into her smug, blushing face as she simpered pathetically and trotted out this well-rehearsed plug. 'The older generation are always moaning about us kids doing nothing but going to discos and listening to pop music and generally lazing about; well, look at this lot, discos and pop music and kids, all helping to raise money for all the worthy causes in the world today.'

Amen to that, Ruthie darling. I had to do something fast or else their totaliser next to ours would look like fever next to a dose of frost bite. So while someone's gran was burbling on about how nice it was seeing kids today behaving like she used to, angelically, I pushed in.

'They got lots of courage too. . . .' I shouted.

'They have?' he queried, finger hovering over the stop button.

'Well yeah, I mean the one over there did her back in yesterday doing high-jump and yet here she is boogying away for fourteen hours, marvellous really. Mind you she is grimacing a bit – there look, yes, definitely a grimace. What courage. . . .'

'Yes . . . yes . . . thank you,' he pressed his stop button and moved on to a couple of second-year boys who still had their roller boots on. 'What do you think of the girls then, you guys? Could you get up at half-past five and get on down with a breakfast boogie?'

While they gaped at him, I called over their shoulders, 'Too risky . . . sounds like a very arduous ordeal for such young kids, girls and all. I mean they're only eleven and eighteen hours of non-stop dancing is tougher than the Olympics. We boys have got more sense. . . .'

He frowned at me and realised it was time to put this particular record straight. 'Let's just remind our little friend here what Ruth Pendryll, the vicar of Berkeley's daughter, said; namely that they do it in shifts and nobody, repeat nobody, does it for more than one hour non-stop. Nobody does it for more than four hours altogether either, folks, which let's face it, is the length of your average disco, so everything's completely under control. . . .'

Then he gave me a dirty look as if to say, 'Beat it!'

'He's only trying to spoil it for us,' said Ruthie GTS behind my left shoulder and as the button pressed on so did she. 'You see, it's also a race: boys versus girls and the first to raise a thousand pounds is the winner. An added incentive,' she added. Whatever that meant.

'Wow, great,' crooned denim dupe. 'Tell me more. Like how's the big battle of the sexes coming on. . . ?'

And off they went. The star attraction was Lucy Gillimore, the Swanswell Dancing Queen. Rumour had it she'd been sponsored for thirty-five quid. She was something else. A fluent mover and gorgeous looking as well. I left with weak knees and a dry mouth.

I just happened to be passing the DJ chatting to DG when I heard him say nice and loud, 'Tell me Des, old chum, how the hell did you land yourself with this cushy little number?'

'They only wanted the best man for the job,' he replied, oozing his deodorant charm. You must have murdered him to get it then, I thought evilly to myself.

63

By another strange coincidence, DJ and DG ended up having a pub-lunch out in the garden of the 'Swan'. I brought out Grisewald's ploughman's and DJ's scampi and chips myself; not because I had any burning desire to act as slave to these two creeps but because I had this burning desire to hear their conversation. They sounded like very old friends indeed.

'Well fancy, I never thought you'd end up staked out in this part of the world,' sighed DJ as I put the plates down in slow motion, and Grisewald shifted uneasily. And oh dear, I forgot the tartare sauce. 'Last time I saw you, you were climbing out of a window,' DJ was relating nice and loud, laughing all over the lawn as I put down the sauce in slow motion. And oh dear, I forgot the pepper and salt. 'What did you get in the end? I forgot? Was it gaol, or did they just sting you for a few hundred?'

Greasewall's eyes nearly popped out of their sockets at this; but being Supercool, he regained his composure almost immediately and chuckled subtly and kept chuckling and tried to keep on chuckling until he thought I was out of earshot. Then he said in a rasping whisper, 'Will you cut that out, you silly bastard? That little runt's worse than MI5!'

Later that evening before I went back to the disco I switched on Radio Severnside to listen to 'Delroy's Dozen'.

'Hi there kids, Shane Delroy here with the top twelve stories, the top twelve hit singles and our top twelve local heroes. Swanswell Comp. forgot it was a Saturday morning to do their early morning thing. Yes sir, while you lazy hounds were sleeping off the night before, Swanswell was, and still is, where it's at! They've been getting on down with the breakfast boogie since six o'clock this morning as part of their sponsored, eighteen hour disco marathon, and it's all to raise money for charity. . . .'

Then the jabbering was interrupted by a disco-hit that

sounded like all the other disco-hits and the interviews came on next: a gran, Ruthie, Ruthie and more Ruthie, even the roller-booters, but no Ducker.

'. . . so there you have it kids, and if you're in the area, like resident in the UK, why not get off the wall, get down on it and start to groove with some Marathon Boogie down at Swanswell Comprehensive. And remember folks, it's all for a good cause. . . .'

In a way I felt quite relieved. If that load of garbled garbage didn't put everybody off, nothing would. At seven o'clock I strolled over the road. I paused as this squadron of scooters roared past, tank-aerials waving in the breeze. The lads had all turned up of course, just to get a look at Lucy Gillimore's legs. Chico turned up with Bernadette Kelly on one arm and a huge cassette recorder under the other.

'Nice piece of machinery,' Gary told him appreciatively.

'Pressie from brother Dean. The only one he couldn't flog.'

Gary blinked at me, but I couldn't be bothered to explain. Davy peered at the cassette. 'Madness?' he grunted. It certainly was.

'Witty lyrics, Ducker, you'd like them,' Chico told me and handed me the machine to look after while he went for a stroll round the cricket nets, and beyond. It weighed a ton and I didn't have much time to play it.

Less than five minutes later, while the three of us were stuffing ourselves with explosive crisps and drowning our sorrows in coke outside the dining room, who should come swaggering up the steps, hands in pockets, fag in mouth, white hair freshly brushed up, but Flash Gordon from Thornbury. He recognised me the minute he walked through the glass doors.

'Hi, sawn-off,' he said, almost pleasantly. 'How's it going then?'

'Fine, fine,' I answered, cool but suspicious. I hadn't forgotten his threat of revenge last week.

He looked round at the classroom doors, the open doors of the dining room with the swaying, bobbing figures, the rhythmical lighting and the booming music. He nodded in satisfaction. 'Thought I'd pop along to see who won the raffle.'

Was that all? Strange reason to come all the way from Thornbury. Raffle? Nobody mentioned anything about a raffle.

'Raffle?' I repeated trying not to sound too surprised.

'What flipping raffle?' blurted out Davy till I tapped his ankle.

'Yeah, sawn-off. Your little raffle. Me and the gang was in Arnold's Grill when some scruffy kids from your place came in selling raffle tickets. Said the draw was at this disco. Nice prizes too. Especially the turkey.'

Whatever he was talking about, it all meant trouble. 'Turkey?'

'Yeah, Baz really fancied a turkey. We'll roast it tonight at the scooter barbecue at Rockhampton. God knows how; he'll probably end up eating it raw. Not that Baz would worry about eating raw meat. He's a right nutter, know what I mean?'

Up till now he'd been looking round me, past me and over me. Now his steely blue fast-bowler eyes twinkled into my twitching face. 'Course, some of the gang reckoned it was a con, a fix. But no,' he shook his head confidently. 'Nah; nobody would try and con Baz would they? Wouldn't be worth it. Once he found out he'd have them raw instead!'

As he laughed, a small army of parka-clad, helmeted scooter-riders marched round the corner of the classroom and up the steps behind him. At the front was Baz, a huge skinhead with eye-liner and fifty earrings. He was in his early twenties, and he wore a 'Madness' tee-shirt. Fair comment.

'Right lads,' he snapped in a deep, business-like voice. 'Tell whoever's running this kids' party that it's time for the raffle draw. You dig?'

He dug the air with a yellowy-brown finger. I suppose I could have just walked away and left them to it. Once Baz found it was a cheap, fourth-rate con it wouldn't take him long to dismantle the dining room and pull the legs of Des Grisewald.

But after all, one good turn deserves another. So I merely held up my hand; genius was at work once more.

'You timed it well . . . er . . . lads,' I told them, having a good look at the so-called raffle-tickets. They were cloakroom tickets with numbers and nothing else. A really cheap job. I gazed at my watch. 'The draw's in three minutes.' Memorising Baz's ticket number I rushed in and found Des. Prising him away from Dinah Spargo I dragged him over to the DJ console.

'Raffle? What are you blabbering about, Ducker?' he wailed until I whispered a few choice threats and horrible possibilities in his denim cloth ear.

'Oh . . . er . . . yeah, the Grand Raffle. . . .' He announced into the mike after 'Thriller' had finished for the tenth time that day. I told him the winning number. 'And . . . the first prize goes to number 359 . . . 359 . . . ?'

There was a slight problem. What sort of prize could I conjure up that would be good enough to satisfy dear old Baz, who even now, after complete confused silence, a gasp then a whoop of delight, was marching through a wide gangway of kids up to the console to collect? I clutched Chico's ghetto blaster tightly and watched.

'Right then, sweetie, where's the turkey?'

'Turkey?' mumbled Des Chicken. He turned to me in panic. I'd forgotten to mention this bit.

'Yeah, puff-ball, turkey.' Baz leaned over the console, grabbed Des by his denim lapels and started to spell out the word; very accurately too. I was loving this of course, but had to interrupt him at 'K'.

'You can have the turkey,' I announced quickly. 'But I must warn you they didn't put it in the fridge straight away, and it's a bit smelly. Well, to be honest, it's very smelly.'

'You mean, it's gone off?' he deduced with great brilliance and let Des go, having lost interest in turkeys and chickens.

Before he could sink his teeth into me I added, 'So the . . . consolation prize is this!'

His eyes grew big as scooter wheels as he saw the ghetto-blaster. He took it readily enough and seemed very consoled. As prompted, Des read out some phoney numbers to make it look good.

The rest of the gang didn't seem very happy about it. As he sauntered joyfully out, holding up his trophy, Flash stepped in front of him. 'Hey, Baz, you said this was a con. What about our turkey?'

'Stuff your turkey, son, ninety quids worth of Sharpie will do me nicely.' And without even asking the shocked, flushed and totally bewildered Ruth Pendryll for a dance, he strode back out and took his army with him.

'Ducker,' she snapped, coming over the instant they'd gone. 'What was all that about? Was that your idea to hold a raffle? A raffle in our disco? And why was that thug rumbling about cons and so on. Ducker!'

Just then another record started up. Prince. Nice and nasty, nice and loud. I cupped my ear at Ruthie's wide-open mouth and heard nothing. Fortunately Davy had managed to have a quick chat with one of the less thuggish scooter-riders, finding out who exactly had sold them the tickets. From the description it sounded like the work of the Burroughs gang who'd been our sworn enemies ever since we pushed them down the science lab steps. Quite clever for them I suppose. I must admit, at first I thought it was yet another con by you-know-who. But I then realised it might be a good idea if I left before you-know-who came back.

I joined up with Davy outside the dining room.

'I thought it was all Chico's doing,' he told me.

'So did I. We owe him an apology,' I said, looking round uneasily as we passed the fenced-in emptiness of the tennis courts.

'You owe him a flipping cassette recorder too,' giggled Davy.

'No sweat,' I waved him away. 'I'll charge it to expenses. . . .'

8. Treasure-hunting, sort of

> *'If his Spanish was as fluent as his English, he would be a linguist of considerable stature, however . . .'*
> Spanish, Mr C. Rhys-Owen

Davy and I teamed up again the next day. It was a cloudy, windy Sunday afternoon: no good for fishing, no good for biking, but being summer, too good to waste lying around inside.

All that week we'd been collecting rubbish and junk for our 'Bring and Buy' sale. We had a fair amount of stuff too, but either the collectors had got the wrong idea or the donors were taking advantage of our good nature, but most of it was 'Bring and Burn'!

'Look, you lot,' snorted Stoney, who was trying to supervise it all. 'It has to be good enough to spend money on, so don't let people unload their garbage on to you. This is ridiculous.'

He picked a pocket calculator out of the box that Bonehead was struggling under. 'I mean look at this. Who'd give you a pocket calculator unless it was totally. . . .'

He had pressed a few buttons, paused, then looked surprised at something and slipped it thoughtfully into his pocket.

'Remember,' I told Davy as we pedalled downhill towards the railway bridge. 'No junk – just good, second-hand material. . . .'

'Yeah, yeah, I know, I was there when Stoney had his moan,' Davy called back, his voice echoing off the bridge like a giant's. 'Mind you, Ducker, our bedroom's a lot emptier these days. . . .'

He didn't know it at the time, but we were off on an antique treasure hunt to Mr Pegson's old house in the High Street. You see, I'd been reading this incredible story in the Sunday Mirror about this teenage girl who'd found a priceless old oil painting in her grandfather's attic. And when I say priceless, for once I do not exaggerate. She'd found a Rembrandt that was worth more noughts than a bubble bath. They showed you this photo of a skinny punk grinning over the picture of a granny in a white hat. If she could do it, so could Ducker the Wonderboy.

Pegson was a natural choice for a treasure hunt: his age for one thing, plus the fact that he was a notorious hoarder. He collected anything: cigarette cards, match-boxes, stamps.

So we strolled up the ramp to his front door like two boy-scouts on bob-a-job. After a ring and a long wait we could hear his wheelchair whining towards us. He didn't seem too grateful either.

'Hullo, Mr Pegson, Davy and I just happened to be. . . .'

'In,' he snapped, all red and whiskery with anger and muttered some short-tempered remark about being 'half-way through'.

He whizzed back into his front room and we then realised he meant half-way through watching a TV programme. He didn't even look at us but managed to listen to both at once – the programme and the con.

'Open University,' he pointed with a stubby red finger. It was a grubby little film about truancy in Glasgow. 'Never too late to learn, eh boys?' he asked, sounding a little more cheerful now that he was back in the swing of things. 'Sociology in Education Foundation Course, unit three.'

Talk about keen. He even had the books on a little table by the ashtray, pipe and tin of horse-manure. The room itself was musty but quite tidy and clean, but that was mainly because Noddy Bright's auntie worked as his home help.

'Got any odd jobs need doing?' Davy asked, bored already. It was a bad question. Pegson's eyes gleamed.

'Tyres need pumping, budgie's cage needs cleaning, garden needs weeding, lawn needs mowing, windows cleaning,' he listed mechanically without even taking his eyes off the screen and the headmaster of some Glasgow comprehensive. 'Old Mrs Bright's too arthritic to get up on the ladder, so she says. Fat lot of use anyway . . . got a mouth like a foghorn and all. . . .'

'Great,' I replied through clenched teeth. 'And when Davy's finished doing all that, are there any old things to sort out – cellars, or attics. . . ?'

Davy gave me one of his dirty looks. Pegson thought about something totally irrelevant. 'You know I used to be a teacher, did you, boys?' We didn't know but that explained his bossiness. 'Taught everything I did: woodwork, science and maths and a spot of English. And the loft hasn't been touched for ten years boys. She's too old and arthritic to get up there too, so she says. Do that place first. . . .'

'First?' Davy gulped as we trampled up the rag-covered staircase. It was a funny thing Pegson having a house with an upstairs, but people said he'd been very stubborn about moving.

'Blimey, Ducker, by the time we do all the things he told us to we'll be old men as well. . . .'

'Better than the dole,' I reassured him and looked up at the door. There was no ladder and it all smelt damp and mildewy. I got on Davy's shoulders, knowing that although he wasn't very tall himself and a bit skinny with it, he was all muscle.

After a few feeble attempts at poking the door open, with him swaying about on the floorboards like a bad circus act, I managed to shove it open and let in light. I pulled myself up painfully and groped around for the light switch. I touched something that obviously was not going to put any light on. Switches don't scurry off on eight legs!

I hung down out of the trap-door like a maggot in an apple and told Davy to ask Pegson where the light switch was. Seconds later Davy came back with the breathless suggestion from Pegson that we needed a torch and he didn't have one himself.

That meant that I was cleaning out the flipping budgie cage while Davy was cycling slowly home and back to get his torch. While Joey leapt frantically round and pecked my fingers, Pegson called out wise old comments.

'We're doomed boy – d'you know that? Doomed. You – you youngsters – you're the lost generation – just look at you – Education they call it? Never – It's no more than minding the shop – baby-sitters, children's entertainers, boy, that's all they are today. . . .'

'If you say so,' I agreed, sliding the clean sand-tray back inside.

Later, quite a while later, I flashed the puny beam of Davy's torch around the roof, fencing with the rafters. The only things of any interest were three large boxes and what looked to be pictures stacked by a beam in the middle. I'd have to shift the boxes to reach the priceless Rembrandts.

'Careful Davy,' I called, lowering the box down to him. 'It weighs a ton!'

I heard a terrifying scream and the box dropping like a bomb on the floorboards. I looked out. When the dust cleared, there was a book on the floor beside the box. About a dozen spiders annoyed at their sudden eviction were trying to get back home and out of the light, and Davy was out in the street.

'No way,' he shouted up, as I spoke to him from the upstairs window.

'You ain't getting me back up there. They're flipping ginormous gert brutes they are. . . .'

Would you believe it? Davy Cole was an arachnophobic! So, while he mowed the lawn, I had to sort out all the upstairs junk. One box of books and a dozen spiders; a second box of books and fifteen spiders; and one last box of photo albums that I thought might interest the old man and one huge spider that had me backing away carefully. Then at last, came the pictures.

They all had these huge, ornate frames that were miles too big and some of them were so dirty and dusty you could hardly see the subject of the painting, let alone read the artist's signature.

No Mona Lisa's smile, no cavalier's laugh and no bloke with one ear missing, but I blew and rubbed hopefully at the corner of the fourth one just the same. As if by magic the R-E-M- appeared. The rest was lost behind the frame. I tilted it to the left; my heart beating drums of glory and endless wealth in my head.

I don't know who that idiot, twit and terrible painter Remington was, but he certainly had me fooled for a minute.

Number five and last but one was a landscape and a very pretty little mountain scene – a watercolour on wood, by someone whose name was also partly hidden by the frame. This one I couldn't shift, but the first three letters C-O and a possible N had me wondering. They seemed to ring a bell somewhere in a distant art gallery in my mind.

Still wondering, I raced to Davy, borrowed 10p and rang up the pub. Being a connoisseur on all things cultural he'd be bound to know.

'Yes, Dad . . . a landscape and the painter begins with C-O-N, I think.' I waited. Yes, of course there was a famous painter. Constable his name was. And yes, he was famous. World famous.

'Would it be worth much money . . ?' I continued. In the distance, like down a long golden tunnel I heard the words. 'You're joking, probably worth thousands, millions . . . I could retire on one of those. . . .'

In a dream I put the receiver down on Dad's repeated question of 'Why', and floated back to Davy. He was fed up to the back teeth by now: the rain had saved him from doing the weeding, and he wanted to go home and tape the Top Forty. We'd done the budgie, mowed the lawn and pumped up the tyres so Pegson was in quite a good mood. Despite the business with Remington, I took a chance and asked him if I could buy the rubbishy landscape as a present for Mum.

'Buy it?' he wheezed through blue-grey fumes of horse manure. 'You can have it for nothing, lad . . . after all, you've done a good two hours' work and I always wondered where those photo albums had got to. . . .'

'I – I'd rather pay for it if you don't mind,' I said and Davy gave me a knowing look.

'I won't argue with you, lad,' he puffed bitterly. 'Being but a poor old wretched pensioner, who fought for his country so's it could pay him a poor, wretched pension, I won't say no to a bit of extra money. . . .'

I gave him five to ease my conscience. I'd brought the four quid and two fifties along with me just in case. I may have had an empty Toby jug, but for the time being less of an empty heart.

Davy had just taken the masterpiece off me to look at it as I was coming down the ramp when some eight-legged art-lover must have popped out of the frame too, because he dropped it on the pavement!

'Careful boy!' Pegson shouted as the one side of the frame broke off and the picture fell out.

'Ooh sorry, Ducker,' fumble-finger stuttered. He picked up the landscape. 'Yer . . . you said it was by a bloke called Constable. . . .'

I could have kicked Davy from here to Bristol. Old man Pegson puffed a smoke signal and his eyes narrowed.

'Constable, eh?' he chuckled emptily. 'That'd be nice

wouldn't it, boys? Me owning a valuable painting like that? Eh? Worth a few million? A nice, tidy little sum to supplement my wretched pension that barely sees me through the week. . . .'

'Constable?' I giggled hysterically and looked at the real artist. This phoney fraud was called Cotman. I nearly put my foot through him. Pegson asked his name as well.

'Shame, never heard of him,' he mumbled, clenching his yellow teeth on the pipe stem. 'My good wife's father bought all those paintings you know. He had a fine eye for good brushwork, so they say. But not that good eh, boys . . . thanks for the five pound. . . .'

'Blimey, Ducker, what are you going to do now?' Davy giggled.

I suppose I could have given it to my mother, but all I wanted at that moment was to get my money back and fast. I sold it next day at the Olde Antique Shoppe in the square. They gave me a quid. Serves me right I suppose.

9. Catching Some Crooks!

'Finds it difficult to concentrate on the task in hand; he finds it easier to concentrate on the tasks of others' Woodwork, Mr Ames

'Good morning Ducker.' A hand clamped on my shoulder in a determined rather than friendly grip. It was Chico and I'd just brought the register back for Stoney. 'You ran off so fast after the disco I didn't get a chance to ask you what had happened to my ghetto-blaster.'

I said I'd thought he'd gone home, then told him to brace himself for some bad news. 'I'm afraid – it was nicked.'

'I know it was nicked,' he retorted, losing patience. 'But I'm talking about Saturday night when I gave it to *you* to look after while I was er . . . otherwise engaged.'

I told him I hadn't seen it since then, but reassured him. 'Davy and I have worked out who the thieves are and we're going to get them in break.'

'Oh really?' Chico leaned back slightly.

'Yeah, really, isn't that right, Davy? Davy?'

Davy was miles away, locked in some rock-video of his latest fantasy. Chico nodded.

'By lunchtime, Sherlock. You and Watson will know where to find me.'

And he left it at that. Davy's always in a funny mood on Monday mornings. He listens to the Top Forty for two hours, tapes it, has his tea listening to it, then spends the rest of the night listening to the tape. The rock-zombie was sitting there now, eyes glazed over and hooded, his mouth screwed up, making fuzzy guitar noises through his teeth and getting the tunes wrong. In between he added drums and cymbals.

'You're sure it was the Burroughs gang who sold the scooter gang those old Xmas raffle tickets? DAVY?'

I clouted his blond curls in exasperation. 'Doov-tish-doov-doov-tish – yeah – doov – doov – tish – two stumpy long-haired kids with flowery shirts and brown eyes,' he said, 'doov-doov-tish! Oh, and a blond dwarf!'

It was important we get that money back for several reasons. We were just about to race off to the science labs where the Burroughs gang had their hidey-hole, when Ruthie and her rival crusade appeared in the doorway of Room Two with Greasewall leering at us behind them.

'How much did you say we raised on Saturday?' she asked in a loud voice.

'Oh, let me see, just over a hundred and fifty quid, I think, or was it more?' he crooned back. 'Yeah, and Lucy Gillimore raising sixty quid on her own, eh? Not bad, not bad. I'll go lock it up in the safe. I don't trust Ducker and his gang, especially now that they must be feeling desperate. . . .'

Desperate? Who was desperate? We were still in the lead – just.

'I bet they haven't all paid in yet,' muttered Davy as he, Gary and I passed the pottery room. As I looked up, I saw a face peering down at me out of the upstairs Home Economics room window. It was Clark, the third year Burroughs. I pointed up at him. He saw me and vanished.

'Round the back, quick!' I shouted, and we stampeded off just in time to catch them tumbling out the back door. We grabbed one and heaved him round the corner in the alley, where no staff could see or hear.

'Right then; where's the money you got for flogging those raffle tickets?' I demanded fiercely, like a TV cop. Clark put his hands in his pockets, leant against the brick wall of the labs and whistled back at me, like a TV crook. 'Don't know what friggin' raffle tickets you're on about,' he replied.

'These raffle tickets!' Gary informed him pulling them out of my back pocket and flipping them round his weasel nose.

'Yeah, and you'd better tell us before we tell Thornie,' Davy threatened, clutching the grubby lapels of the Burroughs hand-me-down jacket and catching six different diseases in the process.

'You can friggin' tell who you like,' said Burroughs looking past us, immune to our threats as well as the jacket. 'You can tell Maggie Thatcher for all I care!!'

'Obtaining money by false pretences is a police job anyway,' I added.

'Don't care if you tell the Pigs either,' he continued piggishly but unworried. 'We'm too young for they to do anything anyway.'

He had us there, the little runt. What should we do? Hang him upside down till the truth and the money dropped out of him? We had to be a bit careful. He did have two big, nastier brothers who, though not particularly fond of him, loved any excuse to get somebody else.

'OK lads, let him go. He thinks we're bluffing,' I said as Davy did let go very reluctantly. 'Let him find out the hard way. . . .'

Clark raised his chin and brushed Davy's fingerprints off his jacket sleeves. Then, hands in pockets, he strolled, ever-so-slowly with a 'Ta-ta slobs' round the corner. I leapt over and peered round the brickwork. Just as I thought he was racing like mad down the path and back into the labs.

'I'll follow and report back,' I told the other two and sprinted off after him. My theory was that he was racing off to his locker to check if the money was still safe and sound.

The bell had just gone, so there were plenty of slow-moving crowds for me to hide in. I saw him haul Spencer Burroughs out of a small group of first years and say a few words that obviously alarmed his scruffy brother. But neither of them went near a locker, or any other hidey-hole in the building.

I followed him to his next lesson in the Art room and even then couldn't be sure he wouldn't sneak out half-way through. We had drama next door, but every time I popped in to check, there he was chatting away to Barnsie and making paper darts to throw at Sandy.

'Now what?' Davy asked, looking and sounding bored, as usual.

'My theory is he'll go to where the loot is stashed away, dish it out and spend it quick before any of us can reach it.'

'I saw this bloke on telly once,' Davy began. 'He did hide some money in the bogs, the bit where the chain hangs from.'

'Too risky,' I scoffed. 'Too many people about. And smokers.'

'Why should we care about money conned from a load of Thornbury scooter kids anyway?' grunted Gary, also losing interest in my detective work.

'Because it's trouble, and we don't want any kind of trouble until we've raised our cool thou',' I said and he seemed reasonably satisfied.

At the end of the lesson I peered round the stage door into the art room to see that Clark was already on his way home. He ate his lunch out of school, or rather, inhaled it.

I followed him unseen and unheard. Like his shadow I tracked him across the yard. Every time he stopped to look round, which he did quite a few times for some reason, I began an instant conversation with the nearest person.

Then to the bike shed and a quick line to a couple of second years. 'Hullo then, love, busy tonight?' I crooned as they blushed and Clark was out through the school gates.

I stood peering round the gate post at Clark as he slipped his paws into his jacket pocket and jogged gently down the hill to the railway bridge. I noted his casual glance over his shoulder. He knew I was hot on his trail yet didn't seem to worry about it.

I was just about to jog gently after him when a hand tapped my shoulder. I jumped a foot in the air.

'It's only me, Ducker,' said Davy when I came back to earth. 'Don't follow him. He's only a decoy, you berk. Look.'

Following the thumb that jerked over his shoulder, who should I see racing up the road in the opposite direction but Spencer: the first year Burroughs. And he looked in a real hurry.

Davy guessed he was headed for home: a pile of junk and bricks in Hinton. We had to run a mini-marathon to keep up with this kid. He should be in the athletics team, I thought. By the time we caught up with him he was tip-toeing down the garden path and round the grey, crumbling stone corner of the Burroughs' den. Why he should tip-toe round his own house I couldn't understand.

Davy dropped on all fours and crawled up to the hedge. He peeped over the top and nodded back to me. 'He's after the loot all right. He's hidden it in the rabbit hutch.'

'Let's wait till he pulls the money out,' I advised. 'And then –'

Whatever my brilliant plan was we didn't need it. The front door clattered open and a woman's voice rasped harshly.

'Clark? Is that you?' It came out and shouted over the hedge and round the front garden. 'Who is it? I know you're there.'

Then it found its victim and pounced. 'Oh, so it's you is it, you little maggot? What you doin' back here at this time of day, I'd like to know? Can't you leave that bloody animal alone for five minutes?'

We both peered over the top of the hedge in time to see the splendid sight of this woman grabbing Spencer by his pointed ears and dragging him away from the hutch and round the corner, cussing him for several different things at once.

'Ow – Gerroff! Ow – I never!'

'You been at my cassette recorder again, haven't you?' she yelled and with her free hand clouted his free ear. Then she dragged him struggling into the house. 'Bloody tape's all over the floor now!'

All he could do was whine the same phrase over and over again. 'OW – gerroff – I never!'

The instant the door rattled shut, Davy leapt over the hedge and I ran carefully through the gateway after him. All we had to do now was open up the hutch, get the loot and go back, now that Spencer was well and truly occupied.

'Uh-oh!' gasped Davy, dropping the hutch roof and retrieving his hand quickly. 'That ain't no flipping rabbit!'

He was right. The ferret threw himself viciously at the wire door of his prison, very insulted at being mistaken for a rabbit. Its claws glinted over the thin metal, claws that looked harder and sharper. In the distance Spencer wailed, 'No – I never!'

'Now what do we do?' I asked as the pink eyes gleamed fiercely at us, his furry head snaking from side to side, eager to get a good bite at our throats. Its mouth was curved downwards like a sad clown, or a shark. In the corner we could just make out the shape of a metal box. 'Go on,' I urged him, realising that time was running out. 'Your dad kept ferrets once.'

'Oh yeah, he did too,' Davy agreed grimly. 'Once and never again. Not after the basket did bite him on the nose.'

I jerked with a quick laugh and started to cough. But he got to his feet and strolled back round the front of the house. I followed him in panic.

'Where are you going, Davy? We can't leave it there, not now.'

'All right, Ducker, you go and get it,' he offered and stood by the front door listening to the continuing struggle.

'She's giving him a right old belting in there. Listen.'

Unlike me, he didn't find Spencer's dilemma at all amusing. Then to my horror, he raised his foot, placed his Doc in one of the wooden door panels and pushed the unlocked door open.

The two of them froze in the hall: her hand drawn back ready for another painful wallop, his arm raised in a feeble effort to ward off the well-deserved blow. She was quite young: mid-twenties I reckoned; a blonde in a white skirt, turquioise blouse, thick make-up, red plastic ear-rings and dirty bare feet.

'And who the hell are you?' she screeched at us. Spencer winced away.

'What are you doing there?'

'We're mates of Spencer,' Davy lied, lazily leaning against the door. 'We was wondering if he needed any help.'

'Help? And why should he need help may I ask?'

'Sounded like he was getting beaten up, that's why. Didn't it, Ducker?' he tapped my ankle.

'Er . . . yeah, that's what it sounded like,' I added. She stood up straight and square, hands on hips, glaring at us.

'Oh did it? Well if you must go listening at other people's doors, poking your noses in other people's business, then hard luck. What I do in my own house. . . .'

She was getting in the swing of this great speech when Spencer seeing his chance, scampered under her arms and burst through the doorway head down. Davy wasn't quite fast enough to get out of her way and the two of them were tangled up for several seconds before she could break free and chase down the road after him.

I was all for having another go at trying to get the tin out of the ferret's cage, but Davy had lost all interest in the idea. He'd gone quite serious and old suddenly.

'Sod it, Ducker,' he moaned. 'Let him have the money. Fancy having to put up with a mother like that. Ours was bad enough.'

And he left it at that. His own mother had gone off a year ago, leaving his dad to look after him and his younger sister. The money didn't seem very important now.

'D'you reckon we ought to do anything?' I asked him as we strolled through the school gates after several minutes of silence. Watson was mowing the lawn by the fish-pond.

'No, course not. Like she said, it ain't really any of our business.'

'Yeah, but she can't go on beating the kids up,' I persisted, like I felt I ought to. 'What about the little ones. It isn't really fair.'

He shrugged and that was an end of it, for the time being.

'It certainly isn't fair, Judas,' a voice agreed sarcastically and there was a tap on my shoulder. It was Chico. 'You told me you hadn't seen my ghetto-blaster since I handed it over for your safe-keeping. So you must have had a blindfold on when you handed it over to our Thornbury scooter friends later on.'

Nothing stays secret in Swanswell for long so I told him the whole story. He blinked at me in disbelief and looked sort of stunned, perhaps because it was the truth, something he wasn't used to.

'But look,' I continued cleverly, 'the next time that gang goes into Arnold's Grill, I give you the money, you take it back, explain everything and they give you your ghetto blaster back. After all you're a Mod aren't you? You go on scooter rallies too. . . .'

He was holding up his hand and nodding politely to shut me up. 'Did you say you gave them my ghetto-blaster to stop them from wrecking Ruthie's disco? Is that right?'

'Well . . . yes . . .' He shook his head briskly. Then he frowned.

'But where is the money then? You sounded like you'd got it back?'

'Ah yes,' I coughed and paused. 'How good are you with ferrets. . . ?'

He gave a little scream and told me quite nastily, that I owed him ninety quid. So that was that sorted out very nicely, and I had an ace up my sleeve.

I'd noticed from the ever-so-loud conversation among the girls in tutor period that Ruthie and friends had several other brilliant schemes lined up: sponsored bell-ringing round all the local churches; a sponsored dog-jog, whatever that was, and a couple of others. I should have started feeling like a loser. But my ace was to simply choose the right moment to tell Ruthie how yours truly had saved her biggest money spinner, namely the Disco Marathon from disaster and defeated the Swanswell Mafia in the process. Out of sheer gratitude she would either give up all ideas of a race, or hand it all over to me as part of my reward. Maybe.

Still there was always Noddy Bright if that didn't work.

'Where d'you keep finding all this rubbish?' I laughed as gently as I could, after we'd all finished jeering at him and his suitcase full of junk. He did seem quite upset all of a sudden.

'Down in the field by the Severn,' he told us as he packed it back in. 'Old Gilpin don't let me go near his farmyard any more. Anyways, I ain't bringing any more in, all I get is laughing and loads of silly comments. Ain't bringing that sword in neither. . . .'

So now he happened to have a priceless golden sword with a jewelled hilt that he hadn't brought in. Stoney didn't help by charging in seconds later and bellowing, 'Get that junk off my desk!'

'Don't call it junk, sir,' said Gary slyly. 'You'll hurt his feelings, look.'

As for our great Bring-and-Buy sale, the team were gradually starting to fill the hall with fifth-hand cast-offs, rejects and breakages that nobody wanted, not even the dustmen. Still when you've got people like Bonehead and Beryl and Cheryl as part of your team you can't expect the Antiques Roadshow.

Stoney popped in after school to see how we were getting on. He was tired but vaguely interested. Not all of the stuff was rubbish. I do exaggerate sometimes.

'When you look round at the cast-offs of consumerism,' he told us, standing in the centre of the hall, 'you realise that there is a direct connection between wanting and wasting, and that we have, we must have, more money than we need. . . .'

He started to wander round the goods, tapping this, kicking that. 'All this stuff is repairable, usable, yet they can't wait to chuck it out. It's as if we're becoming the throwaway society, throwing everything away, wood, glass and paper – slowly throwing itself away until there's nothing left but an open hand, held out for more.'

He nodded solemnly at us, like he does at the end of Social Education. What did he want, a round of applause?

'And looking round at all this clobber,' he continued in the same deep ominous monotone, 'I see even now that something vital is missing.'

We all stopped not-listening and gaped at him. He raised his eyebrows. 'When, on Saturday morning, the doors are flung open and the hordes of bargain hunters come swarming in, what is the first thing they'll want to know?'

'Where it come from?' asked Bonehead brightly, his voice muffled a bit behind his forefinger.

'No,' Stoney corrected with great patience. 'They will want to know how much everything costs. Not one item here has a price. That should keep you busy till the weekend.'

86

And instead of helping us, he jingled his car keys and walked off out into the car-park and his waiting set of wheels.

I gazed round at the junk-heap, then at the team. It was a task of a life-time. And how did we know what things cost? Davy certainly didn't, nor did Beryl and Cheryl and as for Bonehead, whose finger was still knuckle-deep in his brain, if he could price anything within a hundred pounds, he could have it.

'Tell you what,' suggested Bonehead, 'have an auction.'

'Hey yeah, that's a brilliant idea,' shouted Davy. 'They're good for a laugh as well. Everybody loves an auction.'

'Yeah, Ducker, you can be the bloke with the hammer,' sighed Beryl, or Cheryl, clasping her admiring hands together.

'Me? Hold an auction? Talk sense for goodness' sake!' I shouted back, angry at not thinking of it myself. Then I decided.

'I'll tell you what . . .' Davy folded his arms and gave me a knowing look. 'I think the best thing we can do to get round all this . . . is to hold an auction.'

10. The Escape

> *'Works well in class, when under close supervision,*
> *but his homework often shows signs of haste'*
> Maths, J. J. Gonzales

By the time I got home that afternoon I was quite liking the idea of an auction. But there waiting for me in the kitchen doorway was my mother with a message from old man Pegson. I was to go down to his place immediately, the phone-call had said.

'Now what have you been up to?' Mum asked after I'd rung up Davy for reinforcements. He wasn't too pleased either; it was his favourite cartoon.

'Me? I haven't been up to anything,' I protested not liking the 'now' in the question. She gave me a suspicious look and returned to her 'A' level swotting at the table.

Old man Pegson wasn't the problem: it was Joey. He'd escaped! And he blamed us for it. You know, his blue-and-white budgie with the razor-sharp beak.

'Been acting peculiar ever since you cleaned his cage,' he complained grumpily. 'When Mrs Bright opened the door to change his water, he couldn't scramble out fast enough, so she says. And out the window he went before she could catch him; not that she could catch anything with her arthritis. . . .'

He then handed us a large, floppy net from the umbrella stand. There was a pause while we counted puffs of smoke. Then he took the soggy stem out of his whiskers.

'You find him for me, you young 'uns . . . he's the only friend I got . . . I'll give you a fiver when you bring him home. . . .'

And he reversed back down the dark corridor, all red-faced and watery-eyed. Without another word we marched down the pavement to the corner.

'Five quid,' Davy kept repeating in awe. 'That's nearly half his pension innit? Fancy forking out half your pension for a budgie.'

'Not just a budgie,' I elaborated gloomily. 'His last mate by the sound of it.' Davy understood, and kicked my ankle lightly.

'You'd better not take that fiver off him then when we find him.'

'When?' I wailed. 'You mean if.'

'Course we'll find him. You'll be able to spot him a mile off,' he said, optimistically handing me the net. It was torn in several places. Old man Pegson used to collect butterflies with it, years ago of course.

We tried all the obvious places first: the back gardens of the houses down Jumpers Lane just round the corner. No luck there. Not even a butterfly.

'If he's headed for open country we've had it,' I told him pessimistically and handed the net back to him. As we wandered towards the bridge he pointed the handle at a woolly-headed figure strolling across the Castle meadow in a leather jacket. We all met up at the stile.

'Hullo, Murph,' I greeted, wondering what he was doing out there with a pair of large binoculars.

'Second-hand,' he grunted. 'Smart job. No, third-hand. Come off a German U-boat in the war.'

'They waterproof then?' Davy asked. We assumed he was joking. Murphy didn't even twitch. He was in one of his moods; it was either his mum again, or his last girl-friend, or school. Murph tutted softly and then swore, louder.

'What's wrong then, Murph?' Davy asked to put him out of his misery and handed me the net while he examined the glasses.

'Just been chasing along the banks for a kingfisher. Saw this bluey bird in the distance, so it had to be. Would have been the first I'd ever spotted. D'you know what it really was?'

Everybody guessed right. 'Wasn't even a bearded-tit. I ask you – a friggin' budgie.'

Now because he was keen on Animal Liberation as well as bird-watching, we didn't say any more on the subject. He did not approve of birds in cages, even if they did belong to poor old, lonely pensioners.

We climbed the stile quickly and quietly and headed for the banks of the Pill. We left him watching us closely and suspiciously through his U-boat binoculars.

I wonder if he saw us creep on tiptoe across the grass to a willow by the bank, pointing silently at one of the branches. I wonder if he saw Davy stealthily climb up, clutching the net and make his way, like a sloth, up towards the branch. Then a swoosh of the net, a shriek of panic and Davy hung over the water, having dropped the net and lost the bird.

By the time I'd fished the net back out of the Pill, Davy, who must have had pretty strong arms, had hauled himself back on to the branch and was sitting astraddle it facing the trunk. I stood there for several seconds watching Joey flutter off low across the grass with a rowdy flock of sparrows. Then I turned to Davy.

'Hey, Ducker, look!' His eyes were popping out and he was pointing at something across the other side of the Pill. I couldn't see anything, so he beckoned me up beside him. Once I'd scrambled up and perched, nervously, in the fork of the branches I saw it too. Or rather the two of them. Des Grisewald and Dinah Spargo walking amorously hand-in-hand along by the bank about fifty yards further down.

'Wonder what they been up to?' he asked. I gave a low wolf-whistle. The two lovers hadn't seen us, but we both jumped down before they could. Fascinating though this all was we still had to catch the budgie.

It was hopeless: we chased him over the meadow to the castle wall, where he perched on the ivy, chatting up sparrows and quite pleased with his outing. We tried calling his name. That did not work. We tried to shoosh him over to the houses. In the end we just called him all the names that came into our angry heads. By the time we returned to the stile and Murphy, we were exhausted. So was he; he hadn't laughed so much in all his life. He didn't help by jeering 'Go-ee budgie,' every five seconds either!

He pointed lazily at a blue and white bird flapping over our heads to perch on the gutter of Pegson's house. Then he perched on the upstairs window ledge. Then the downstairs window ledge. All we had to do was open the front door and let him in, it was that easy in the end. But Cole the Hunter was itching to get his own back and use the net.

Every time he pushed the net carefully towards his quarry it hopped on to the wooden handle, chirping insults. Davy tried to shake him off into the net, but the bird just fluttered away and perched somewhere else. Again the net slid slowly towards him, again Joey hopped on to the handle. 'All right then you clever little . . . budgie!' Davy roared in exasperation and grabbed the bird in his hand. Bagged it at last!

Old man Pegson nearly jumped out of his wheelchair with joy when he saw the beaky, blue and white face of his best friend poking out from Davy's careful grip. He whizzed across to a jar on his table, as Joey began to leap about his cage – glad to be home, we hoped.

'Go on, boy, take it,' he insisted after we waved away his generous Duke of Wellington. 'Go on, after all . . .' he added mysteriously, 'you boys done me more good than you could ever imagine. . . .'

I thought he meant finding his feathered friend. I could

never have guessed what he really meant. But he was so insistent I had to take it.

'I won't argue with you, sir,' I answered, ignoring Davy's boot in my ankle, 'but we'll put it to a worthy cause. Our little appeal for the . . . er . . . for the school.'

'Oh, that business,' he puffed, unimpressed. 'I read about that in the papers. School kids never had time for that sort of thing in my day,' he continued as we backed away politely. 'Too busy learning, that's why.'

As the lesson ended we slotted the net back in the umbrella stand. 'Fat lot of use you were!' Davy spoke to it like a friend who had let him down.

On the way back from Pegson's, all Davy could talk about was the romance of Des and Dinah. I was only mildly interested. I had other things to worry about.

'We could blackmail him,' shouted Davy as we free-wheeled downhill, towards the bridge. I told him Dinah was over sixteen as he drew level, looking at me instead of the road. 'Yeah, but out in the open like that? In public? That ain't right, surely.'

'Come on, you guys, that's really uncool,' I answered. 'And besides who flipping cares? I mean Dinah Spargo . . . for goodness' sake. . . .'

Just then the echo of a car horn roared off the bridge's belly like a juggernaut. Who should it be, but dear old Des Grisewald himself in his third hand MG. We waved at him cheerily, two-fingered of course.

'Anyways, that five quid you took off Pegson,' he reminded me, still annoyed that I'd pocketed it, 'that means you now owe Chico only eighty-five quid.'

Then it was my turn to wave 'cheerily' at him, as the pub appeared over the brow of the hill.

He was right. I could have used that fiver myself. I could also have used the raffle money the Burroughs gang conned out of Flash and his gang. Soon, however, I was to get it back in the most amazing way.

It was about a quarter to six. I was being extra good doing the washing up while Mum went upstairs to revise her 'A' level stuff. Halfway round a tea-cup I suddenly felt this tug on my jumper. I turned round and nearly jumped on to the draining board,. There staring up at me as he tugged at my sleeve was the blond-haired, glass-eyed ugly face of young Spencer Burroughs.

'You,' I gasped. 'How the hell did you get in?'

'I did come through the back door of course,' he explained. The door was still half open I noticed, so I went over and opened it a little wider, as a hint. He didn't take it. He didn't move. I checked quickly round the cupboards to make sure nothing had been nicked. And I saw that he was holding something behind his back. He walked over to the sink.

'It weren't my idea to cause trouble,' he began in this dull, flat voice that never changed. 'That was our Clark. He hates you – and Ruthie Pendryll.'

'Thanks for telling me,' I said sarcastically, knowing this already.

'And Coley – and Chico – and Thornie – and Bleachie – and –'

'Yeah, yeah all right,' I cut in with raised hands. 'So he hates everybody. He must take after your mum,' I added trying something out. He didn't reply. 'That was your mum we saw the other day wasn't it?'

I was beginning to feel a bit uneasy. He kept staring at me with those empty grey eyes, with a sort of half-puzzled, half-scared look. Then at last the mystery was solved. With a clang and a jingle he put this metal box on the kitchen table in front of me.

'There!' he announced proudly. 'I did bring it back.'

I gaped at him and swallowed hard. Spencer Burroughs,

by all accounts the most devious, the meanest, the least trustworthy and least likeable of all the gang, had brought back the loot conned from the scooter riders. I didn't quite know what to say.

'Don't tell the others,' he stuttered.

'No, course I won't!' I gasped. 'But, tell me, why did you bring it back?'

'I – I don't want to do bad things . . . not all the time,' he stammered. 'I want to do good things for a change. When you stopped our Fabia from giving I a going over, I thought I would do you a good turn back, like.'

Was he serious? Was his mother really called Fabia?

'We ain't as bad as what folks say we are,' he continued in the longest speech anybody had ever heard him utter. Normally he acted like a deaf mute. 'Our dad ain't anyway. He's all right he is. When he's off the booze he is anyway. . . .'

'Well, that's, er . . . that's really terrific, Spencer. I'm very grateful and very impressed. Yes.' I didn't know what to say. 'I'll make sure it goes to a worthy cause.' I thanked him again feebly and eased him away from the drawers full of cutlery and steered him towards the back door.

'I don't care what they others think,' he continued, stopping stubbornly by the Welsh dresser. 'I do think the swimming pool's an ace idea. I love swimming.'

'Good, glad to hear it, Spence. I'll let you know if we can use you for anything. . . .'

'I'll do anything I will,' he said. Only the words were enthusiastic; the voice, the face stayed as blank and un-moving as ever. 'I – I never done good things yet.'

I opened the metal box and looked thoughtfully at the loot: 50p pieces, pound coins, 10p coins and some shiny, golden quids. Must have been ten, fifteen quid or more. Hardly worth putting in a box. But he had brought it all to me. I still couldn't believe it.

'I'm going to run away, I am,' he said loudly, as if scared that I'd lost interest in him. 'I hates it here – everybody fighting and rowing. I've had enough. I always gets the blame.' He nodded in determination. He stepped forward to get more of my attention. 'I wants to go to Africa.'

He announced it suddenly with a furtive glance as if this was some big deal confession. I tried to be polite and fascinated by all this. 'Oh really? What, to go and help the starving kids?'

'No,' he said surprised. 'To go and help the elephants. It ain't fair the way they do shoot they elephants. Just for the ivory and that. Did you know there's forty thousand different muscles in an elephant's trunk?'

I was a Save-the-Whale fan myself but I saw his point. He was so desperate to please, I realised the only way to get rid of him would be to let him do his good deed, congratulate him on it and hope that would satisfy him. So I let him finish the washing up.

I stood behind him watching closely, making sure he put the crockery and cutlery on to the draining board and not into his jacket pocket. It was like watching a robot. In between dipping into this warm, soapy shipwreck, he'd tell me more about Africa and his elephants and rhinos, or the hunting habits of the lions. He'd read this book from the library he said. I bet he still had it too, with the ticket holder ripped off and everything. Sad when nobody trusts you.

He took ages, but when at last he shook the suds off his stubby red fingers, I patted him on the shoulder.

'By the way, what are you going to say when the others find the money's gone,' I asked out of genuine concern. But he'd seen to that very nicely. He told them Davy had taken it! Then I had yet another brainwave. 'There is one more thing you can do that would be a great help,' I told him. He turned to me and almost smiled. 'The next time your little gang plans to mess us about, just let me know.'

He shrank back. 'Eh? They'd kill me if I split on them.'

'Ah, not if we used a code-word,' I informed him calmly. 'If the gang are planning anything, just say the word "ferrets" to me and I'll understand.'

I tapped the side of my nose. He looked slightly more puzzled than usual. Perhaps the idea was a bit ambitious. Then taking the metal box he emptied the money on to the table. My father's voice called me from the bar. I went into the corridor to answer, felt a draught in the back of my neck, returned to the kitchen and found it empty. The back door was half open. It was like I'd been talking to a ghost.

As I counted up the money and prepared to put it in the little polythene bags, I felt quite warm inside. What with Pegson's budgie and Spencer's washing up, I'd managed to do two good deeds in one day. A record. Whatever Ruthie thought about the Swanswell Swimming Pool Appeal, it was certainly making a better person out of me. As long as we beat her.

Dad called angrily a second time. I then realised that I'd been talking to Spencer the way Thornie used to talk to me!

11. A Helping Hand Gets Bitten

'Basically good-natured, but he needs to try harder'
Mr M. J. Stone, Tutor

When I finally wandered slightly dazed into the pub, we had one customer and Dad wanted me to open a new box of crisps while he went on serving this one customer. It was old Dill of course, who else? When the door opens at six o'clock you see him on the mat in the starting position.

'Dad,' I began, having thought long and hard about this nagging problem. He stopped moving and stiffened. 'You remember you once said that good people can never be bad, but bad people can sometimes be good?' He relaxed and remembered. It was after a TV news story about two skinheads who'd pulled an old man from a burning car in the motorway.

'Yes, vaguely. Why?' He started to wipe the bar-top.

'Well, if the bad can be good sometimes, why can't they be good more often and end up being good, all the time?'

'If I knew that,' he answered after a brisk shake of his head, 'I'd be Prime Minister. Or the Archbishop of Canterbury.' He chuckled and glanced up at Dill who was examining the foam on the top of his pint.

'Yeah, but if they can be good sometimes, what makes them bad in the first place?' I continued, feeling my brain winding itself into a slow knot.

'If I knew that I wouldn't be working in this humble pub, I'd be. . . .' He paused and realised he'd cracked that joke already. 'Maybe it's their upbringing, or their environment. You know, surroundings. After all, if your father's a burglar,

97

your brother steals cars and your mother's a shop-lifter, where would that leave you?'

'In the Burroughs family,' I thought to myself, but I did feel slightly less confused.

Maybe that was Spencer's problem. Deep down he was a good kid: a bit devious, crooked and nasty, but basically he was all right. It was just being in that family, being knocked about by everybody, that brought out the worst in him. And who can blame him? Perhaps, if somehow the adults could be persuaded, or forced, not to bash their kids, or at least lay off the little blond-haired one, then Spencer might yet be saved.

Next morning, feeling flushed with noble intentions, I got out of tutor period to see Des Grisewald. Believe it or not, I had swallowed my pride to seek his help. He was supposed to be good at things like that – pastoral care they called it.

Stoney was doing 'How good a son, or daughter are you?' on yet another worksheet. Well, I knew I was the perfect son: a bit troublesome now and then, but whose heart was in the right place, and so worth every grey hair.

Des was in the youth centre with a cloth in his hand trying to clean a coke ring off the snooker table. Dinah Spargo stood in the corner, arms folded and grim-faced. Just as I trotted up the steps I heard her say, 'No, Des, I told you – I can't.'

Seeing me, he nearly dived into the nearest pocket. Then he turned and smiled feebly; with a slight jerk of his head at Di he hinted that she remove her embarrassing carcass to some other place. She stayed.

'Hullo, then, Ducker,' he said with a tinge of sarcasm. 'How are the seven dwarfs getting on with raising their thousand?'

'Fine, fine,' I lied politely and decided to stay cool no matter what he said, or did. 'But, er . . . I have come about something else. A social problem.'

'Oh really. Hey Di, Ducker's got a social problem now. Bad breath is it?' Having failed to get rid of her, he was now trying to get rid of me.

'I mean, what happens if you know about this family, where the adults beat up the kids?' He threw the cloth down dramatically.

'Which family?' he said instantly, looking me in the face for a change.

'Let's just say "a family". I mean, what happens if you know the mother wallops one of them?'

'Which family, Ducker?' he repeated nastily.

'All right, all right. Supposing, just supposing mind, it was the Burroughs family. I mean . . .'

'The Burroughs family,' he nodded sourly. 'Again. So supposing I told you Mrs Burroughs died two years ago?'

I gaped at him and wished I hadn't bothered. He smiled knowingly and went on: 'You mean Fabia? Mr Burroughs' new friend? Well, yes, she probably does lose her temper now and then, and lash out. It's not an easy job trying to look after that lot.'

'But she was picking on him for something really trivial and giving him a really hard walloping for it.' I was waiting for him to ask me for the boy's name but he didn't. Instead he turned to Di again.

'This is the new Ducker. The good little schoolboy who promises to do his best now and forever. Who sticks his nose into a thousand different places where it's not wanted and pretends he's doing his good deed for the day.'

'What are you on about?' I shouted.

'Oh come on, Ducker,' he shouted back. 'We know all about your little feud with the Burroughs gang, you and Coley.' He explained some more to his audience, 'Ducker and his wolf cubs are going to build us a swimming pool. Anybody can join in you know. Except those who can see through him, of course, like Ruth. Oh, and the Burroughs gang. Oh no, we can't have them, can we? They're far too common and scruffy.'

I just could not believe this. He was accusing me of being a snob, a phoney, a con and everything else. And he hadn't finished.

'So, not satisfied with that, you're now into splitting up the whole family. You want a custody order brought in, do you? So the kids can get put into care and farmed off to some nice little middle-class families like yours, so they can behave like decent people? You know, well brought up, well-behaved, decent kids who treat kids like the Burroughs gang like dirt. I mean you really want to go that far?'

'Yeah, Grisewald, very clever,' I simmered. 'And don't bother spitting on that wood again. You've eaten through half of it already.'

I left it at that. Of all the bastards! He was only saying all that to show off in front of adoring Dinah, of course. Apart from the fact that he hated my guts. Just because I tripped him up at last term's football match.

Still seething with rage, I bumped into Chico in the corridor. He'd only just arrived, having missed the bus.

'Ah, there you are,' he said obviously. 'On my way past the totaliser in the foyer I noticed that yours is still on four hundred. This means you have not used the twenty-five donated by the cricket fans. If you have no idea what to do with it, I shall relieve you of it and leave you owing me only sixty-five quid. That's ninety minus twenty-five. Ninety for the ghetto blaster, Ducker?'

I was only half listening, enjoying a mental picture of kicking Des Grisewald in the next football match; if I could wait that long.

'Yeah, yeah, I do understand, Chico, but, er . . .' I looked up at him to see if he was still angry. 'How would you like to do me a small favour first?'

He stepped back, looked over his shoulder, pointed at himself. 'Me? You want me to do you a favour?' he quipped sourly, still angry. 'This is a turn up for the books. I mean, first you scorn my assistance, then you give away my prized possession to a load of strangers in order to save the enterprise of your greatest rival and in between you keep half the money off the totaliser. Then you ask me to do you a favour! It is confusing, Ducker, very confusing. I can't work under conditions like these so I think it's time we re-considered our business partnership. . . .'

'How do you fancy being an auctioneer,' I put in quickly. 'You'd love it. You'd be superb. Fast talking, getting money out of people? On Saturday?'

'You heard the news about the girls' bell-ringing on Saturday?' he asked, pretending not to have heard what I'd said. 'Correct me if I'm wrong, but they do seem to have cleaned up three hundred quid between them. But you see, Ducker, they know what they want and they know what they're doing. They had that poof from Radio Severnside there, didn't they? Publicity it's called, Ducker. And it worked. Success, Ducker. Now why can't you manage something like that?'

I was just about to give him a very rude answer when the door opened and Stoney towered over us. There was a long snigger from the class behind him. 'I do wish you two love-birds would hurry up and finish your squabble. For some reason the class is finding your row more interesting than my lesson.'

There was a little cheer as we both entered, and Chico, to my disgust, got a round of applause from the girls, Ruthie clapping loudest of all.

Could things get worse? When the bell jangled ninety minutes later for break, the lads all rushed off to the tuck shop and youth centre. But I stayed put. Or at least I tried to. Two minutes had passed and the formidable figure of Miss Bleach, complete with blue rinse and red plastic glasses, stood beckoning me from the doorway.

'Come here, young man,' she boomed in that deep, preacher's voice of hers. 'Mister Thorne wants a word with you, in his office, now.'

The 'now' was barked out like a parade ground command. I jumped to it, trying to work out what it was all about as I marched. Miss Bleach was IF's form teacher. She taught Humanities. She worshipped Thornie. She hated me ever since I answered her back once when she was standing in for Sutherland, our own teacher. She had called me a 'silly, little boy' and told me to grow up. I grew up hating her.

Thornie was sitting at his desk with his executioner's face. The door closed on the noise of break funnelling down the corridor to his office. Miss Bleach was Spencer Burroughs' form teacher. Miss Bleach and Des Grisewald used to run a summer camp for Rangers.

'I have just received a serious complaint about you,' he announced. She sat primly at the edge of the green armchair, listening like a poodle.

I stood and shook like a wet bloodhound. He sat back in his swivel-chair and revolved like a rear-gunner.

'What's this about you spreading malicious and dangerous rumours; rumours of child assault, baby battering et cetera?'

Des, whatever terrible things I said about you in the past, none of it did you justice. He waited uneasily for my reply, she waited eagerly for my death sentence.

'I was only trying to help,' I croaked desperately, hoping he'd believe me.

'Help? How exactly were you trying to help?' he said without moving his lips and with Miss Bleach's parade ground voice. He raised his eyebrows at me to explain.

'We actually saw him getting hit: me and Davy Cole, that dinner hour.'

'And what were you doing at the Burroughs' house during that dinner hour?' she asked.

'I, er, we, er . . . thought he'd stolen something of ours, but he . . . hadn't.'

'There we are headmaster,' she elaborated trimphantly. 'That poor family is the scapegoat of the whole district. If ever anything goes missing or gets stolen they are suspected immediately.'

'More often than not, they stole it,' grunted Thornie who had read his papers even if she hadn't. 'Anyway, it's a long leap from one quick-tempered outburst to an accusation of child-battering.'

'I haven't accused anybody of child-battering,' I said, daring to raise my voice at him. 'But I bet it's happened more than once.'

'This is not a betting matter,' he snapped back. 'You're way out of your depth. God knows what your motives are but you're wrong, you've made a big mistake.'

'I've been round Ivy Cottage personally, Headmaster; when Spencer was playing tru . . . was going through that difficult phase. Mr Burroughs was perfectly charming. He's an intelligent and articulate man, even if he is workshy and fond of drink. There's a lot of love and affection in that family and I don't see why they should be constantly victimised by the rest of the community. . . .'

'You haven't noticed any bruises I suppose,' he asked suddenly, turning to look at her. She sat bolt upright with surprise. 'It happened once before you came here,' he continued. 'The girl, Heather, now in the fifth form. A couple of years ago this was, but we could never prove anything. That was before our Fabia appeared on the scene, too.'

'I still think he ought to write a letter of apology to the whole family today.' She regained her composure to add this poisoned post-script.

He stood up at last and nodded. 'We'll check this out and you will keep quiet about it. You could make things ten times worse for Spencer and for us. And for you, come to think of it.'

He nodded again to her as she swept out with a swish

and a crackle of static. The noise flooded back in like water over a cracked river bed. I had to stay and write this letter at his desk.

'I'll dictate it for you,' he said gruffly. 'Dear Fabia, sorry I interfered but I'm only young and didn't know any better. The next time anything like this occurs I will consult my Headmaster who knows much more about these things than I do. I shall not breathe a word of this to anyone, but if I do I am quite willing to explain it all personally to Mr Burroughs.

Yours sincerely, Ducker.'

He lit one of his pathetic brown, hand-rolled sticks, blew smoke across the desk and picked up my letter. He read it through, and nodded once or twice with satisfaction. Then he folded it in half and popped it in his inside pocket.

'I shall see she gets this personally,' he announced. I thought he was going to throw it in the bin after I'd gone. The bell went and he gazed past me at the door. I mumbled, 'Thank you, sir,' and left.

I was amazed that Thornie had taken my side; at least I think he did. Anyway, thank goodness he didn't take the idea of any letter of apology too seriously.

12. The Great Swanswell Auction

'Watching him work in a group is more an experiment
in human behaviour than ordinary science'
Science, Mr Newton

Stoney liked the idea of the auction and of my holding it. I
hoped he'd think me too young, or useless and do it himself.
But he said he'd be better off keeping an eye on things in
the hall. Sort of overseer. I could see what he meant. In the
end we did manage to collect some valuable items, and no
doubt they would be more than a temptation for some
people.

There was this flashy BMX bike propped up next to
some smart white garden chairs, a lawn mower, a sleek
cricket bat with stumps and a toy pedal-car with 'Starsky
and Hutch' emblazoned on both doors. All of it was good
value for money.

'Stoney's dead right,' Davy muttered philosophically.
'Fancy giving away stuff like this to us lot. They must have
too much money. . . .'

'What d'you reckon, Ducker,' Davy told me as we both
stood envying the girls' totaliser in the foyer. 'Spencer
Burroughs came and asked me if he could bring his ferrets
to the auction! What a nutcase.'

'Yeah,' I grunted. He didn't know about Spencer's visit,
or the raffle money which was still in my desk drawer in my
room. As for Spencer's ferret, it rang a bell somewhere but I
had no time to remember why. I was too busy praying that
the auction was going to be the money-spinner I'd hoped
for.

'By the way,' he asked later as we sorted out auctionable material, 'you know how to do it, do you?'

'Relax, Davy, all is under control,' I lied, 'I just wish we had someone else to do the bloke with the hammer.'

'Honestly, Ducker, I can't see what you're getting so worried about,' he reassured me. 'Usually you love shouting your mouth off all over the place.'

Later that evening Dad introduced me to all the regulars who had been to auctions: cattle auctions, antiques, cars, the lot. In the end I was quite an expert and Dad was almost impressed by my brilliant organisation.

'You mean it's today?' he blurted out at ten o'clock on Saturday morning. I nodded. 'But when's the viewing?'

'The viewing?' I echoed emptily. He rolled his eyes.

'Yes, the viewing. You heard what Roy Streeter said last night. You must give the customers a chance to examine the goods first. To whet their appetites so to speak. You should have had the viewing on Wednesday.'

'Oh that?' I shrugged it off. 'They can view it on the way in.'

'Oh can they?' he concluded sourly. 'And what about the catalogue? You have got a catalogue I suppose. No auction ever takes place without a catalogue.' I shrugged again. 'Otherwise how on earth are they going to know what's up for auction?'

'They'll know once they see it on the way in, at the viewing,' I told him confidently. He slapped his forehead.

'No viewing, no catalogue,' he listed. 'You really have organised this auction superbly. You'll be lucky if anybody turns up at all.'

'Everybody knows about it,' I told him. 'After all, the Swanswell Swimming Pool appeal is famous round here.' He did not dispute that fact. 'Anyway, don't worry, Dad. It'll be the most memorable auction ever.'

It certainly was. By eleven o'clock we had it all sorted out into lots, with junk items ready to get sold off in bulk. In fact we ended up with quite a lot of lots. A 'lot' is the term the experts use for items under auction. Being an expert, of course, I used it.

I was on the stage behind the lectern. I had a toy hammer Davy had picked out of some wooden banging-frame. I feld dead nervous, naturally, but also slightly chuffed to be up there, mastering the ceremonies. We'd put chairs out and everything. Then the press arrived.

It was the creep from the *Gazette* who'd nearly ruined our marathon. 'Hi kids,' he said uneasily. He had a camera man with him again. 'Still at it, eh?'

Eh? At what, I wondered. This bloke was a jinx. However I soon had other things to worry about because the hall started to fill up quite quickly as people wandered round doing their 'viewing'. G-man stayed lurking at the back and every time a new wave of customers swept in, he floated to the back of that, like sewage on the tide until he was standing in the glass doorway.

'Good morning ladies and gentlemen, boys and girls, teachers and parents and friends of Swanswell Comprehensive,' I began and Gary tried not to laugh and Davy had to turn away. 'I hope you'll all be very generous and remember that it's all for a good cause, yes, all this. . . .'

'Get on with it young 'un!' snapped a rat-faced old man in the front row who'd been casting his beady little eyes on every item of value, even the BMX bike.

Davy obeyed by wheeling the lawn mower on to the stage.

'Right, then . . . starting with, er . . . lot number one, the lawn mower! Good as new, blades sharp, roller smooth – now what am I bid . . ?'

All faces were eagerly turned towards me. Then old rat-face put up his hand.

'Two pounds . . . that's all I'm offering, what with my

old age pension and everything, two pounds is all I can manage . . .'

And he turned in his seat and grinned at the other old man next to him who squinted like a mole.

'Two pounds?' I gasped at the stunned audience. 'You must be out of . . . must be joking, sir, with all due respect . . . but as the ladies and gents must have noticed, the roller's worth two pounds on its own. . . .'

'Been after a good, cheap mower for years, ever since I retired,' he told the first four rows. His mate nodded moleishly.

A muffled voice shouted three pounds and Stoney gave Davy a dirty look. Gary shouted four.

'Five pounds, our young 'un, and I'll be damned if I fork out any more for that old wreck,' he wheezed and turning in his seat looked round to dare anybody else to outbid him.

'Any more?' I appealed in vain. 'No? Surely? What? Nobody? . . . Gone to that old . . . to the gentleman in the front row,' I muttered bitterly as he rushed forward to grab his prize off the stage. Any more old age pensioners and we'd be cleaned out for ten quid altogether!

Bonehead wheeled the almost good-as-new BMX on to the stage. It was worth fifty quid at least. As I started the bidding I could hear shouts and growls and could see what looked like a scuffle as Thornie came through the glass doors to sort out the trouble. It was quite a scrum, too, and sort of scuffled itself through both glass doors out into the foyer.

The bike was now doing really well. I'd reached fifty-two quid when this tough-looking bloke in tee-shirt and jeans came marching down the aisle clutching the hand of a wide-eyed blond boy.

'How about a hundred and forty quid?' he shouted very loud and pointed at me.

'Thank you, sir,' I accepted gladly. 'Any more advances on a hundred –'

'I ain't bidding for it, am I? That's what I paid for it last Christmas,' he shouted round at the puzzled, shrinking bidders. He pointed at Bonehead. 'That's my boy's Christmas present and you, Thickhead, can bring it down here, fast!'

Stoney took a deep breath and got to his feet. 'Excuse me, sir – is there a problem?' he asked, like a polite shop assistant.

'Problem? Who said there's a problem? I'm just getting my boy's bike back and that's all.'

There were some shouts of protest from other bidders. It was a popular lot. 'Can you prove this is your boy's bike then, sir?' asked Stoney.

'Prove it? Why should I prove it?' the thuggish parent half-laughed, half-snarled back. 'He had it nicked from our front garden didn't he, last night? I could ask you how it got here in the first place. . . .'

Stoney looked down at the finger prodding away at his chest. After prod number five he looked up. 'Look, if you can't prove this bike is yours then you might as well cut out the shouting and sit down with the rest!' Stoney shouted suddenly like an angry maths teacher.

There was a little cheer to back him up, but for one incredible moment it looked as though Mr Stone was going to get a punch in the head. However, the little blond boy, who'd been digging in his pocket, pushed his way in front of his dad's huge tattooed forearms and peeped, 'I – I got the number in my diary, look – the frame number,' and he handed it to Stoney, who took it, almost disappointed at not getting involved in a punch-up with thug-knuckles, read the number and clambered up on stage.

First he had to ask the kid what the number was again, then he lifted the bike up, looked, said in a loud, hollow voice that everybody in the silent hall could hear, 'I don't believe it!'

Then he handed the bike back, patting the kid's blond

head and actually apologising to his charming father. In the same breath he pointed a finger at me.

'I think that this Auction is closed; You and your crooked bunch of cronies have got some questions to answer, right now.'

Before even question one got an airing though, several people had got angrily to their feet to take a closer look at the other lots. Down the spinning, multi-coloured, echoing tunnel of my latest nightmare I heard voices shouting, 'Here, that's my garden chair!' Someone else shrieked, 'Our Nigel's pedal-car!'

Stoney was facing me, but his twitching ears were picking up the messages from behind. He actually went white. The blood drained from his balding dome into his beard like a thermometer on ice. Very slowly, he turned, hardly daring to look. But yes, Stoney, I'm afraid you're right. You are looking at chaos, real chaos. Everybody was on his or her feet grabbing various items and claiming they'd been stolen. Those items that weren't stolen were conveniently grabbed to save the inconvenience of paying for them. Clothes and bedlinen were torn in half by eager women who wanted more. Furniture didn't take the strain either and broke its legs or just collapsed. Books were ripped into blizzards of confetti as bookworms turned into vicious snakes. People were pushing then falling over each other, legs kicking in the air. It was as if the whole world had gone stark staring mad. No wonder Stoney stood with his back pressed against the stage, not daring, not able to move.

The team had all taken safety on the stage, staring in horror at the riot going on before them. Noddy, Bonehead, the twins and Gary.

'Oh, Ducker,' Beryl moaned, clutching my arm. 'What are we going to do?'

'Why did you have to go and nick it?' keened Cheryl, clutching my other arm.

'I didn't nick it, you stupid cow,' I shouted as people even started to argue over the drama hall chairs. 'Would I sell it in public if I'd nicked it?'

'Well, where the hell did it all come from then?' shouted Gary, trying to make himself heard over all the racket.

'I don't know, do I? Unless . . .' Of course, it had to b 'It's somebody setting us up for some reason.'

Davy had at last struggled through the struggling mob to get up on stage with us. 'Come on, Ducker,' he wailed almost in tears, he'd been laughing so much. 'Let's get out of here quick!'

'Where to?' I screamed as we legged it across the art room.

'Hi-jack a plane to Beirut,' shouted Gary overtaking us. 'That's the only place we'll be safe. . . .'

Even half-way down the school field we could still hear the shouting and screaming. We looked glumly at the fence that was blocking our escape. In desperation we climbed over it. Suddenly I remembered. 'Yeah, we must have been set up,' I told them as Bonehead jumped down on top of me. 'The press were there like they were expecting trouble, right, so someone must have tipped them off.'

But the others were already jogging up the farm track, over the hill and out of sight of the school. We ended up sitting at the edge of a meadow in the shade of an oak tree. The grass shimmered with flies and insects. Perhaps it wasn't so bad being an insect. All you had to do was climb up stalks of grass, eat and breed and watch out for spiders and big feet.

I straightened up, put my hands behind my back and prepared for the saddest moment of the whole enterprise. Yes, I was to bid farewell to my loyal troops; I would miss them all right. The strength and sheer masculinity of people like Gary, who even now was kicking the heads off buttercups. The energy and determination of Davy Cole, who had his penknife out and was slicing up a twig. Then, Beryl and Cheryl, the charming chubby duo, huddled together, gazing up at me with their glassy blue eyes. I wished I could remember which one fancied me – the better-looking one I hoped, but I wasn't sure which one she was. Noddy Bright, who had tried so hard to be useful and had taken so much stick for his pains; he was already fast asleep dreaming of Sutton Hoo. And last of all was Bonehead, and you can guess what he was doing. I don't know why I bother sometimes.

I rehearsed a speech mentally for a few seconds, then at last addressed the assembled veterans thus; 'Team – I'd like to thank you for all your valuable help and support and stuff in this er . . . valiant enterprise. It was, as they say, nobly done, and everything and so therefore . . .' I looked up. Nobody was listening.

'I'm packing up this bloody lark right now!' I shouted and sat down on a large, painful root.

'Thank God for that,' grunted Gary, squinting in the bright sunlight.

'No way!' rebuked Davy angrily. Throwing down his stripped twig, he jumped to his feet, 'I don't know about you, but I didn't get all soaking wet, cut, bruised and knackered doing chariot-races, piggy-back, collecting stuff for the auction, earning three hundred and sixty quid just so I can give it all to Ruthie Pendryll. No way. How can you say you're packing it up? You're supposed to be the leader. Come on, show some guts.'

'Yeah,' chorused the twins, giving him a little patter of applause. 'Yeah,' rumbled Bonehead, glasses flashing blindly at me.

Noddy woke up with a start, 'I never stole your bike, honest, I. . . .'

Somehow the sight of Noddy staring up at us in horror, as if we were the thug-knuckled dad of his nightmare, cheered us up so much and so quickly that we forgot how much trouble we were all in ourselves. They all started going over the funny bits of the riot, until waiting for a pause I had to remind them:

'Yeah, well, someone has to go and face the music, you know, take the rap, and well, because I'm the leader of the team, it'll have to be me. . . .

Er, as for the great Swimming Pool Appeal, the future of that depends on what's left of me after the music has been faced, you know. . . .'

I felt quite proud of them, well most of them, as we all trudged up and over the farm track which wound its way uphill and round the bend past the school field. At the road, we all parted company. I told Davy I'd see him in the evening and I started to amble apprehensively across the car-park.

The school was locked up but the caretaker was waiting.

'There you are, Ducker,' he called with cheerful mischief. 'They been looking for you – all over the place – you and your little gang.'

'They?' I asked. He stood with his hands on his hips trying not to laugh as he remembered. Clockwork sat obediently at his heel and listened to the total.

'Mr Thorne of course, and PC Blackwood and half a dozen parents, plus that young bloke from the papers. They wanted a photo of you.'

I bet they did. I bet the police wanted a picture of me too, for their rogues' gallery. 'They all thought you went back to the "Swan", and that's where they all went. Your dad's been really busy this morning.'

'It wasn't anything to do with me you know,' I tried to explain. Clockwork looked up at his master to see if he believed it.

'Try telling that to the judge,' he joked and started to walk off to his bungalow. 'Never-mind – they say

Dartmoor's quite nice in the summer. . . .'

Luckily, when I got back to the pub, after a very slow stroll, the troublemakers seemed to have gone. There was a young couple and a load of tots trying to wreck the see-saw and the climbing frame, and a bloke reading a newspaper, presumably waiting for his lunch. It was ten past two after all.

Dad didn't ask me how the auction went, which meant he already knew all about it. Instead of a telling-off he handed me a chicken-in-the-basket. 'Here, do something useful for a change,' he commanded brusquely. 'Customer out there wants this on his table, in front of him – not all over him, or on the grass. . . .'

Everyone was a comedian suddenly! When I got outside the reader put down his newspaper and beckoned to me, pointing rather rudely at his table-top. As if I was that stupid! He didn't look very hungry either, or happy. Still it was a hard life being a headmaster.

'Your chicken in the basket, sir,' I said, sounding like head waiter. I unwrapped the cutlery from the paper napkin and laid it out neatly on the white metal top, unfolded the napkin and was about to place it on his lap, when he snatched it away angrily.

'Yes . . . yes . . . all right, I can manage. . . .'

I turned to tip-toe away, but he called me back, and it wasn't for a tip.

'Sit down,' he ordered and to my disgust proceeded to eat with his fingers; starting with a quick sample of those delicious chips.

'Ducker,' he paused suddenly and looked up. 'I might as well call you by your nickname, as everybody else does, including the police. . . .'

'Oh sir,' I whined as he licked a greasy finger. 'It is Saturday!'

'Saturday's as good a day as any,' he responded quickly.

Now for some chicken. The leg pulled away with a silent, succulent rip of white flesh. I was starving and this was slow torture. 'Some headmasters are lucky,' he was saying. 'Their kids let them have the weekend off. But oh no, not Swanswell. They have to be doing things on a Saturday: marathons, discos, so-called auctions; things on which I have to keep a paternal eye, just in case. . . .' He placed the clean, drying bone on the edge of his plate. 'Just in case there's a mass outbreak of theft, or the odd riot – you know, the usual things which happen when free enterprise gets out of control and sows the seeds with which capitalism will eventually destroy itself. . . .'

'But sir, we wouldn't try to sell things we'd stolen in the same area, would we? That's not free enterprise, that's suicide. . . .'

'Yes, yes, Ducker. I'm not daft, nor are the police. We've gone through all that already. Your form tutor was delighted with the way things have turned out I can tell you. But it has all been sorted out, and all the stolen goods returned to their rightful owners. It would help though if you could tell us how all the stolen, borrowed, or misplaced items turned up at your auction, and why. . . .'

'I can only think it was part of a plot to discredit us, sir,' I guessed out loud, sensing he wasn't too hostile then. 'It would have been our most profitable enterprise, sir, and they were trying to ruin it. . . .'

'They,' he repeated meaningfully with raised eyebrows and soggy chip. 'Who exactly are they? Surely you don't mean the girls. Things aren't getting that bad round here are they?'

I shook my head. There were only two possible choices of auction nobbler and I didn't really like either of them.

He stretched out his hand, grabbed mine and shook it firmly. 'Good try, Ducker. Now just forget the whole thing and I won't hold it against you.'

'You mean . . . forget the appeal, sir, the whole idea of the pool?'

'Everything! No more appeal, no more fund-raising, in other words no more trouble. Peace will return to Swanswell. Saturdays will once again be days of rest and recreation.'

I felt betrayed. I sat there completely speechless. He decided to put on a bit of pressure. 'Your parents aren't very pleased either, by the way. Your father even went as far as to ask me what he'd done to deserve a son like you. . . .'

I looked up as he wiped his grey moustache clean of grease. 'So I told him that at least your intentions were good, even if disaster dogs your every move. . . .'

'It'll still be curfew,' I muttered, well and truly cheesed off. He looked a bit surprised, but oh yes, from now on it would be in by five and bed by nine! What a summer this was going to be. There was a long pause as he took a frothy swig out of his ebony bucket of Guinness, pulled out his cigarette paper and tobacco and started to roll his own.

'Would you like the umbrella up, sir?' I ventured, creepily, spotting this oversight. The sun was very hot now. He shook his head irritably. He was obviously a man who didn't like being fussed over. Perhaps all widowers were like that, I wondered sadly.

'Have you ever heard of the theory of the Four Elements?' he asked vaguely. I shook my head politely, relieved at this change of subject. 'Perhaps that's next year.' He licked the paper and rolled himself a lolly-stick of tobacco. 'Anyway, the theory goes that in human communities, like school for instance, there are four elements: the first element always does what's right without being told; the second element does what's right after a bit of persuasion; the third element does what's right only after you've scared it to death; and the fourth element, ah yes, the fourth element never, ever does what's right. No matter what you say or do, it will go on doing wrong and will continue to do so until Doomsday. Understand. A cynical little theory when you come to think about it. . . .'

I nodded, feeling privileged rather than enlightened. He pointed his faglet at me. 'Which are you, I wonder?'

'Er . . . borderline?' I suggested carefully. He seemed to agree and cupped his hands round the flame of his match, even though the breeze was a feeble one. 'Never mind – I'm still on your side – for the time being. . . .'

That was very reassuring I must say; and as he looked across at the tots pushing each other off the climbing frame he waved his match expansively. I took the hint and left.

13. Calling it Quits,
or trying to

*'A boy of his intelligence should set an example
to others'* Mr M. J. Stone, Tutor

Not surprisingly I had to spend two whole hours of that
Saturday afternoon clearing up the debris after the auction.

I told Davy about Thornie's ultimatum. He was very
stubborn. 'You'd better not,' he warned. 'Never mind what
Thornie says, if you so much as look like you're going to
hand over our money to Ruthie, I'll flipping break your
arms.'

This was almost taking loyalty a bit too far. 'Leave
Ruthie to me,' I told him quietly. 'Tomorrow I shall pop
round to the church and make her an offer she cannot
refuse.'

'Oh yeah?' he giggled. 'After she chucked you last term?'

'Ruthie Pendryll still fancies me like mad,' I informed
him. 'It's just that she's pretending like mad that she hates
me.'

'Who's pretending?' he laughed and we wandered across
the car-park to his bike resting against the wall.

'A word from me and I'll have her eating out of my
hand,' I declared bravely. Thornie was locking up the
school doors behind us. He looked very tired, though I
can't think why. He obviously liked being in three different
places at once.

'Come round our place for tea,' Davy invited wisely. 'It
would get you out the way for a bit.'

I accepted readily and watched Thornie climb wearily
into his Ford and chug off home to his lonely cottage in
Stinchcombe.

When we got to Davy's place, his dad was stripped to the waist in their small garden planting lettuce seeds. His dad was a larger replica, with grey hair, curly of course and a side-tooth missing, which made him look like an old key when he smiled, and he smiled a lot. But he was much quieter than his son, and worked on farms repairing machinery.

We had supper in front of their colour telly. My dad was still happy with black and white; something which always made me go bananas.

Our place was tidier than theirs though, which wasn't saying much. Their terraced cottage had been in a bit of a state ever since their mother walked out twelve months ago. His sister didn't help much, expecting the two men to wait on her hand and toots. She was either draped over the furniture playing Pak-man, or trying to teach their dog Shane some party trick and telling everybody he ought to be on television. Shane was a tiny mongrel like Watson's clockwork dog, only lazier and not so clever.

I spent a hectic and exhausting two hours there: teasing the dog, teasing Donna, trying to beat them at Pak-man, and then up in the men's room Davy suddenly announced he had something even more spectacular in store for me. Picking up three of the fifteen odd socks lying odourously round the room, he rolled them up.

'Now then, Ducker, my little failure, watch this. Something else you can't do, I bet.'

And to my amazement he started to juggle with the three odd socks – not very well, but he could keep all three in the air for about ten seconds at least.

Shane the Wonderdog loved this piece of real entertainment and kept leaping up like a dolphin to try and catch one of them. All he had to do was wait till they landed on the carpet. What a family! They could form their own circus. Then I thought of this busking idea that somebody had had earlier as a scheme to raise money for the appeal.

'How about a street circus?' I asked him suddenly. 'To raise money, I mean. You and the dog and your sister all dressed up, like clowns maybe, plus a couple of other acts. Yeah. How about that?'

'Rubbish, Ducker!' he assessed bluntly and dropped two socks on to the dog's grinning face. Shane grabbed one and began to worry it like a rat. I glanced at my watch.

'My God,' I shrieked. 'Three minutes to curfew! Ta-ta. Think about it, you two. You'd be an instant wow, honest!'

And without pushing my latest brainwave any further I thundered down the stairs and out of their front door, down the garden path and along the road, making it with only seconds to spare.

The curfew wardens had deserted their posts however. As I crept through the kitchen door no-one was around. I could then hear muffled voices from upstairs – discussing number one problem son, no doubt.

I had a quick look round to see if there was anything I could do: washing up, sweeping the floor, cleaning the windows. Then I noticed one of Mum's poems lying modestly on the unit. I picked it up and read it.

> 'The foreign swallow on the
> wing
> Wants only

The warm call of our mother sun
> Once only
> The surrounding green for
> breeding.'

Yes, well, very nice too, if you like that sort of thing. It was certainly better than the week's before. I memorised it quickly. No sooner had I done this than Dad came bumbling down the stairs red-faced from his latest row, saw me and dived into the cellar to sort out pumps and the lager barrels, he said. Mother followed.

'That's very good, Mum,' I congratulated creepily,

pointing down at the week's masterpiece. 'You ought to send it somewhere. . . .'

'I ought to send *you* somewhere instead,' she quipped icily and picked up a book from her 'A' level pile on the table. She had the exams on Monday. No wonder she was in such a bad mood. Being used to taking hints, I bowed my head and went upstairs.

Next morning I was up nice and early to be helpful round the pub and ready to sort out Ruth Pendryll. For a start I went to church with my mother, telling her how good her poem was on the way. I sang nice and loud too, like I used to when I was in the choir before my voice went all croaky. And I hope all the seventy-two old ladies of the congregation appreciated it, as well as the Rev Pendryll and his daughter.

Afterwards, when we filed past, shaking his hand to celebrate his certain entry into the Guinness Book of Records for preaching the most boring sermon ever, I made my move.

'Your Dad's sermons get better all the time,' I said to Ruthie.

'How would you know?' she queried suspiciously. 'I haven't seen you here for ages.'

'Why not make a habit of it?' I suggested in my usual cool, chat-up tone. 'Like this afternoon, that is, if you've nothing else on. . . .'

'You know very well I take a Sunday School class in the afternoon,' she reminded me coyly, going all pinky, fluttering her eyelids and obviously delighted at the thought of getting it together again. She always was a push-over. I stifled a yawn and turned it into a smile of admiration. 'Will four o'clock be all right?'

'By the tower?' I clarified and confirmed. She was almost too excited to nod. 'Don't be late mind. Curfew starts at five.'

She thought this was an amazing joke, laughed loud and

long and beamed at my mother knowingly. 'Ducker, it was never me who was late,' she giggled another reminder.

What a transformation; mortal enemy, deadliest rival one minute and queuing up to be my latest the next. Such is the power of the chat. That Sunday afternoon she was all togged up in her grooviest outfit; blue denim dungarees and pink blouse, as well as a hint of lipstick and turquoise eye-shadow. You know, she wasn't bad looking. But she always had to go and spoil the effect by opening her mouth.

She suggested a stroll over the bridge and along by the Pill; our favourite route once.

'You know about yesterday I suppose?' I asked. She sniffed a quick laugh. Nothing stays secret round here for long. 'Thornie had a phone call from Mrs Thatcher. Our Swimming Pool appeal was a threat to world peace, so could he persuade me to pack it in. Well, naturally, if the choice is between world peace or a swimming pool, I had to choose peace. . . .'

She was dead keen on CND too. 'Never mind,' she replied, with an edge in her voice as we tilted down the steep hill from castle to bridge. 'It must have been fun while it lasted.'

'I suppose there's not much point in doing your appeal now is there?' I dared to ask. She began to get the message and her hand stopped knocking accidentally-on-purpose against mine.

'Well . . . I think eight hundred and fifty pounds is a very respectable sum. We made another fifty cleaning cars yesterday, by the way.'

By the time we reached the water I realised she'd had the cheek to add our total to hers.

'Surely you haven't forgotten the challenge you took up?' she asked in a voice getting all steely and defensive. 'Never mind what Mrs T. said to Mr T., you lost, Ducker. You and your little bunch of thieves and vandals were well and truly hammered.'

This sounded like as good a time as any to play my trump card. If I could control myself long enough to say it. Some cows looked up from their grazing and gazed idly at us as we passed by on the opposite side of the river.

'Listen, Ruthie, let me just tell you that instead of grinding your Christian heel in my loser's face, you ought to be shaking my hand, no, you should be flipping kissing my boots, you owe me that much!'

The arms folded, the eyes rolled under the turquoise shadows.

'Who stepped in when those scooter-yobs were going to wreck your disco after the Burroughs gang had sold them phoney raffle tickets? Who even had to give them Chico's cassette recorder as a peace-offering? If it wasn't for me, your marathon disco wouldn't even have raised a laugh and they'd be still trying to dig you out of the rubble. . . .'

'So?' she goaded with curled lip. I could have pushed her in the Pill. 'So you've obviously got a conscience after all or maybe you just did all that, knowing you'd lose and hoping to pressurise me with it after!'

'For Christ's sake, Ruthie, what have you got against having a swimming pool?' I shouted, jumping up and down, back on square one after all.

'If you're going to blaspheme I'm going!'

'Bloody hell, Ruthie, can't you be normal for once?'

'If you're going to swear, then you obviously must have run out of ideas and we have nothing further to discuss,' she snapped, turning on her heel.

'You haven't listened to a word I said,' I shouted after her. She stopped and waited for me to catch up. 'You still owe me one, whatever my motives were. Did I save your biggest money-spinner or not?'

'Well, that's just it isn't it?' she said, hands on hips, green eyes beaming down at me. 'Your motives have been rotten from the start. Everything we've done has been legal, honest and decent from good, honest motives –'

'Trying to show me up? That's a great, good motive!' I tried to stem the flood. No chance.

'But you and your bunch of swimming pool pirates; everything you do is accompanied by violence, vandalism, petty crime, gang warfare – God knows what – It's like the Mafia raising money for a Godfather's birthday.'

'You were just jealous because I got so many kids interested in raising money. You wouldn't have done all this if I hadn't had the idea in the first place.'

'Look,' she retaliated coldly, putting on her GTS stance to regain her composure. 'You're quite right, I didn't like your swimming pool idea from the very beginning. The whole thing was about greed and selfishness.'

'Oh sure,' I laughed, red with fury. 'I'm so greedy and selfish I kill myself raising money for a pool that hundreds of kids and adults can use. Why, even you could have used it, if you'd promised to keep your mouth shut once you were in there.'

'Oh cheap-cheap, you sound more like Chico every day. But that's not surprising since you have to get him to run things for you.'

'Chico Marks hasn't helped us raise one penny!'

'Like the cricket match with those very strange odds?' How she found out about that I don't know. But nothing stays secret in Swanswell. 'Not once have you ever showed genuine concern, or decent morals about anything,' she continued, now within spitting distance.

'I know right from wrong, if that's anything to do with it,' I defended myself, getting soaked at the same time. I kept Spencer Burroughs as a real secret.

'You were supposed to change,' she explained with sudden calmness. 'After your classic report you told everybody you'd change. Now instead of changing you're trying to buy Thornie off, bribe him with a thousand pounds.'

'D'you really believe that? That if I raise a cool thou'

Thornie will pat my head and say "What a good boy are you, give me that report and I'll rewrite it." Blimey, Ruthie, you don't know Thornie.'

'I know you though,' she lied hastily. 'You don't know right from wrong at all; you just know the difference between getting into trouble and not getting into trouble.'

'Same thing!' I said, to annoy her. It worked.

'Oh no it jolly well isn't,' she shook her head till her lank hair swung across her face. 'And it's time you learnt it. So I'll tell you what you have to do.' Deep breath and brace yourself time. 'You must present me with your three hundred and fifty quid in third year assembly and tell them you're doing so because it's the better cause – For local charities!

She was joking, or delirious with rage. I raised a hand. 'No, no hang on.' I paused. 'I'll get Chico to do it and he can say he was told by God who appeared to him in a dream.'

She was purple by now and ready to strangle me – for my own good of course. I turned to leave her at the foot of the hill. 'Anyway, you haven't won at all,' I surprised her. 'Because we haven't finished yet. Oh no. The swimming pool will be built and with *our* money! Your five hundred quid will come in very nicely too. Now if you'll excuse me, Ruthie darling, I have to go, because there are five minutes to curfew. . . .'

And with that I was off up Castle Street with her prancing after me shouting warnings, threats, insults and 'wait-a-minutes.'

So much for diplomacy. This was now total war. A fight to the bitter finish. And may the best boy win!

14. Trouble-makers!

'Contributes actively enough to the life of the school, but I would now prefer some more useful contributions'
Mr R. Thorne, Head

On the way home, Des Grisewald chugged past me in his fourth-hand MG, going in the opposite direction. No doubt off to pick up his sweetheart for another stroll along the river bank. Ruthie could call me all the names she liked, but I wasn't as bad as some of her idols.

The crazy thing about Ruthie and her rival appeal, the thing which irritated me more than anything, was that if we'd teamed up together, we'd have raised a thousand pounds in less than a fortnight.

Monday morning found Chico in another bad mood. This time it wasn't my fault. Bernadette Kelly had given him the push.

'She said I was too fast!' he complained nice and loud and not without a hint of pride. The lads sat round eagerly in Room Two waiting for gory details. 'She called me fast and she's a year older!'

'Catholics,' I assessed shrewdly. 'She thinks you're only after her body.'

They all turned to gape at me: Chico's gape widest of all. 'I *am* after her body,' he confessed unashamed. 'Who d'you think she is – Ruthie Pendryll?'

A great raucous laugh and they turned to see if she had heard. Then it was my turn to blush. 'By the way, Ducker; commiserations about your Swimming Pool Appeal. When are you going to hand the loot over to Sexpot?'

More raucous laughter. Ha-ha. I waited till the end of

tutor period before I told him the news. 'Chico, before I screw my finger up your nose, get one thing straight, and spread the word: we haven't stopped raising money for the pool, got it?'

'If you ask me you haven't even started,' he quipped back as he packed his bag with girlie magazines, pop magazines and chewing-gum from his locker. 'Anyway, you can't double-cross Thornie now. The whole idea was to get into his good books, wasn't it?'

I closed his locker door for him with a slam. 'When we do get our pool, you're going in first, fully clothed!' I promised. Actually, it turned out to be Gary in the end, but there you are. He stood up slowly. 'Ducker, you are beginning to confuse me again. Your boss says no more appeal and yet you're still having an appeal?'

'Ah, but not inside the school; it goes on outside school, got it? And on second thoughts, don't tell the whole school. We'll surprise them,' I warned.

'You'll flipping surprise me and all,' he said, swinging up his bag and preparing to march. 'But anytime you want some good ideas, ones that work – don't hesitate to ask somebody else. . . .' And he giggled his way quietly to the first lesson of the week.

When I informed the team about my intention, Noddy stated fearfully that his dad wouldn't let him; Beryl and Cheryl cooed, 'Do you think we should?' like a pair of nervous turtle doves; Gary had gone to play snooker, Bonehead picked his nose and Davy said: 'Never mind that, we got a score to settle first. . . .'

'No more trouble, Davy,' I said firmly.

'Too right. By the time I've finished with the little bastards they won't be able to cause any. . . .'

And he hauled me back out of Room Two that break into the corridor. I managed to call back, 'Careful, Bonehead, you'll get brain-damage!'

Then once again, the two of us had Clark Burroughs cornered round the back of the school. Really, it was that two-faced little gnome Spencer we should have been grilling.

'You can't prove nothing!' sneered Clark, chewing an extra pink tongue of gum at us and leaning against the brickwork, hands in pockets.

'Oh no, jughead?' snarled Davy, doing his Starsky and Hutch bit. 'Well, you left your footprints on the BMX, the cops said!'

'We wore gloves, so how could we have?' Clark was really confident. Then wrenched himself free from Davy's grip. 'Anyway, Coley, you're the one who nicked our flipping raffle money, so don't go calling us thieves! You had that coming to you.'

'They dumped the stuff in the auction to get their own back,' I explained to Davy, who was looking very puzzled suddenly.

But then he grabbed Clark by his pointed ears. 'Even though I don't know what you're on about, you lying, thieving hound, you'd better make this the last time you cross us, Burroughs,' he warned. And that was the end of the interrogation.

Davy wasn't sure why I wanted Spencer either, but we had him trapped round the back of the terrapin just before the end of break. As he was only in the first year, and a very small first year, I thought I'd better handle him instead.

'What've I done?' he wailed as Davy stood on his foot.

'We thought we'd like to thank you personally for helping wreck our auction,' I told him.

'I never,' he told me.

'And as for promising to tip us off you two-faced little toad. . . .'

'I did tip you off,' he retorted. 'I did tell Davy the code

word. I did tell him I was bringing ferrets to the auction. That was the code.'

'That's right, Ducker,' Davy interrupted. 'He did say something about ferrets. I told you as well.'

'You did?' I said blankly. They both nodded at me. 'He did?'

'Yeah, I did,' he affirmed in a louder voice as if I was the idiot now.

'Well done, young Spence,' I congratulated, and patted his bony head. 'Just testing, just testing.'

I smiled at the two of them, coughed quietly and strolled off round the terrapin as the bell went. Davy chased after me.

'Now what you up to?' Davy interrogated. 'Why did Clark say I stole the raffle money? How come Spence is on our side using code words and rubbish like that? What's going on, Ducker? Behind my back as well. . . .'

I promised to draw him a picture in art explaining it all, which, for some reason, didn't please him.

Tuesday morning Mr Robert Thorne B.Sc, Dip. Ed., B. H. (Beleaguered Headmaster), took our assembly himself. He told us that for several reasons the Appeal had to stop – not cancelled, he said; postponed until the summer holidays – almost the same as cancelling it. The reason he gave was 'O' and 'A' level candidates whose future, after all, was at stake. He must have been pretty embarrassed to put it as politely as that.

As the whole third year looked at me, then Ruthie, he asked if there were any questions and as usual nobody bothered. Chico was in some sort of day-dream, probably still nursing a broken heart.

'Why don't you do as the old man says and leave it to the hols,' Chico advised on the way out. I shook my head firmly.

'Business as usual,' I told him. He smiled.

'Oh it's business now is it? What sort of business?' he asked as the herd trampled around us.

Over the past twenty-four hours I had been working on this really brilliant idea. The best yet. Even he was bound to see that. 'Busking?' he shrieked with laughter, though nobody took any notice. 'I do not believe it. There are the girls cleaning up hundreds over the weekend, with even better ideas lined up for next week and all you can think of is . . . busking?' He bent double with mirth. Ha-ha. Then he straightened up ready with more kindly advice. 'Do as he says, Ducker, my happy blunderer: wait till the summer holidays. Not the coming ones – the ones after that.'

He had a point though, the rat. How else could we raise the necessary six hundred pounds or so? The girls had used up all the good ideas between them. Back in Room Two I tried to get some people interested in the 'Swanswell Street Theatre', a name which occurred to me half-way down the corridor and sounded quite good. Noddy asked me if I wanted to see his Viking sword and I told him gratefully what he could do with it – take it to the museum or something!

I had a coke in the youth centre to drown my sorrows, but there at the foot of the steps was Chico. Didn't he ever give up?

'Can't say I noticed the kids rushing to be buskers,' he began. I corrected it to 'Street Theatre' for him. He ignored it. 'Ducker, the only buskers I ever heard of making money, were those who donated their bodies to science after they'd died of meths. Now for a good idea. Ready?'

I was ready. I was also desperate. As long as I didn't have to put on a mask and rob the post office I didn't care.

'Why don't you come in with me and make a video nasty,' he said proudly. My turn to laugh. He didn't like it of course. But why he persisted with this idea I could never understand.

The next day we had a really interesting humanities lesson. 3L, our class, has humanities the same time as 3F, the second worst class in the school. The two classes were next to each other and by some stupid piece of designing, to save space apparently, the only way into Room Eight, where 3F were, was to walk through Room Seven, where we were. So it was that ten minutes after the start of my favourite lesson and the story of the American Plains, the door burst open and without a word of explanation or introduction, Miss Bleach barged in pulling Clark Burroughs after her.

'How dare you!' she bellowed so that even Mr Sutherland cringed. 'How dare you call me that in front of the class! We'll see what the Headmaster has to say.'

'I never called you nothing!' he shouted back, trying to struggle free. 'I was talking to Sharon Chapman!'

'Don't you lie to me!' she boomed, as our class put their pens down and sat back to watch and listen. 'Besides, it doesn't matter who you meant it for, how dare you use such language in school!'

And she cuffed his ear with a sharp crack. To our great disappointment, she then heaved him outside and down the library steps to the foyer and Thornie's office. There was a great jeer from the lads.

'Here, sir,' shouted Chico, 'what was all that about then?'

'Yeah,' called Murphy from the other side of the class room. 'Let's go and ask 3F!'

He got to his feet to stroll next door, but Mr Sutherland advised him to remain sitting. It didn't matter, because 3F had started to infiltrate our class on their own. Already people like Barnsie and Jammy were wandering through, hands in pockets, bidding Mr Sutherland a polite 'good morning, sir,' and 'how's it goin then, sir?'

'Why was old Bleachie murdering Burroughs then?'

shouted Murphy from across the room. The class fell quiet to hear.

'Hardly surprising,' said Jammy. 'She told him to spit this chewing-gum out so he called her a. . . .'

'Get back to your lesson!' Mr Sutherland commanded, knowing that he had enough problems, with 3L, let alone reinforcements from 3F.

'What bloody lesson?' Barnsie replied rudely. 'We ain't got no teacher!'

He laughed around at the amused 3L while Jammy started to chat up Dawn Devonshire. Suddenly Belinda Brown jumped to her feet and opened the window.

'He's running out of the school gates, he is!' she shrieked and instantly the whole class was on its feet, charging over to the windows, struggling for a good viewpoint. Squeezing through, I got there just in time to see Clark Burroughs walking quickly across the car park and through the school gates. A voice called him back. Clark turned, waved a V-sign and ran. Then Thornie appeared running after him, across the car park and out through the gates. Some cheered him, others cheered Clark.

'Get back to your tables,' a voice pleaded with us, so we turned and did as we were told, more or less. But order was soon restored. Miss Bleach came marching back in and shouted at everybody, including, it seemed, Mr Sutherland, who was told to 'stop all this noise at once and get back to your work!'

I couldn't resist this chance to lean across to Ruthie and say, 'Not fair is it? People always pick on Burroughs.'

'Because he asks for it, that's why,' she retorted, defending her favourite teacher. 'And don't pretend you're not enjoying it.'

'If I was Clark I'd sue her for assault,' I added. She ignored it. Perhaps I could appoint myself as his lawyer, and add the fees to our total.

It was this event which helped break the ice between me and Jammy. As we queued up for lunch, he told me the word, which wasn't as bad as I thought it would be. We found out later that Burroughs got suspended for a few days. Jammy was dead keen to join in the 'Swanswell Street Theatre'. He even claimed it was his idea in the first place. Let Chico enjoy his adolescent fantasy about video nasties, the Street Theatre was going to be the money-spinning hit I had been waiting for.

15. The Swanswell Street Theatre

'He has a lively interest, in this subject, judging by his constant whistling in class.'   Music, Mr Nichols

You may be wondering why I haven't mentioned Jammy before. The reason is that both of us had disastrous reports and as a result the school decided the best thing to do would be to separate us. So Jammy went into 3F. He was so furious about it, he didn't speak to me for seven days.

Now I needed his help. Like most trouble-makers he had more than his share of talent. He was a red-hot violinist for one thing and just the sort of star attraction we needed for our Street Theatre. He could play absolutely anything and was worth paying for, when he was in the mood, that is.

'I shall be there,' he promised. 'But if anything goes wrong and we get done by Thornie, it was all your idea.'

'Thornie won't even know it's us,' I explained. 'Because we'll be wearing masks, that's why.'

This brilliant idea was Sandy Sanderson's actually. There was a load of masks hanging up in the art room that he'd made for one of Miss Silverberg's drama spectaculars; they were good masks too, moulded ones. Jammy tried one on the minute he arrived because he and I wanted to see Sandy about the posters he'd promised us.

He may have been a Trotskyite and a lech', but he was all right was Sandy, our hippy, weirdo art teacher.

'You're incredibly naive,' this white mask said to me. 'You mean to say that if a load of kids start to appear in the Market Square playing silly baskets trying to raise money for a school's swimming pool, that Thornie will never guess it's you! If he doesn't work it out in half a second I'll eat my chin cushion.'

'Anyway,' I told him, 'Saturday morning's an athletics match, so he'll be up in Gloucester all day lending his support. By the time he finds out it's us, the money's in the bag. . . .'

I reached up and tried a mask on too. As we waited for Sandy to come back from the pub, some fourth-year gossips came trotting in at full tilt, leaning slightly forward, arms folded, small mincing steps, mouths wide with surprise or news. It was usually worth a listen.

'He never,' said Gossip number one. 'You're lying. He never. . . .'

'Cross my heart and hope to die – he did ask her to flipping marry him,' said Gossip number two.

'He never – that's just his excuse to have his way.'

'She accepted anyway – can you believe that?'

'She never. Oh she never did. Her dad'll kill her if he ever finds, if it's true, that is. . . .'

'Her dad'll kill him you mean – he's eight years older than her.'

'So? Look at Charlie and Di? Don't make no difference.'

'What? Old man Spargo ain't the Duke of flipping Edinburgh though is he? she squawked. 'With his wicked temper, he'll cut his head off!'

And off they went, trotting it out in small steps and snippets of information, having conducted the whole conversation in front of us. These masks really worked.

Sandy and Des Grisewald came back five minutes later. Des took one look at us two and left Sandy breathing cider all over us, but heaving out some posters. There were nice ones too: 'Roll Up to the Swanswell Street Theatre', with the date and venue, the market square. One poster for

Streeter's shop, one for the board by the castle, and one for Arnold's Grill. As he handed them over a thought struck him.

'You, er . . . have told Mr Thorne, and the, er . . . Old Bill know about it too, I suppose?' he checked cautiously.

'It's not illegal, is it?' Jammy asked.

'Well, it always pays to let them know beforehand, you know; makes them feel wanted,' he added, chortling cheerfully in his beard.

'Yeah, it's all been seen too,' I reassured him. Jammy looked surprised.

Despite everybody's total apathy at first, things were now taking shape very nicely. We had twelve kids doing eight acts: including Davy's sister Donna and their acrobatic dog; Benny MacMenemy's performing rats, Davy's juggling and an astonishingly good ventriloquist act with Beryl and Cheryl as the dummies. Even Chico offered his services. He reckoned he could do magic.

'Like making other people's money disappear,' I said to put him off.

'Oh-ho, so you're resident comedian are you? Don't tell them jokes, just tell them about your appeal, that'll have them in stitches – if they believe it that is. No, no, Ducker. You've seen my "Spot the Ball" trick.'

'Not that one again,' I groaned and turned away. In Room Two Davy was trying to juggle with apples and dropped two of them straight away. 'Who's going to pay money to watch you do it wrong?' I complained.

'I'll pretend it's deliberate, a clown job.'

Then he started moaning about Sandy's superb masks and how it was difficult enough without a mask, let alone wearing one. He had a point there I suppose. With only two days to go I mentioned it to Sandy, who, resourceful as ever, suggested clown's make-up. It would still be a disguise and there was enough white make-up in the drama box left over from last year's production of *Godspell*.

We used the drama hall to rehearse. I had struck up a deal with Miss Silverberg that we could use the hall and count on her support provided we put on the same show at the end of term. If Thornie was to ask any questions, then she'd merely say we were rehearsing for our show, even, once at least, in the streets of Berkeley!

Chico appeared during a break – well, more of a break-down. Davy had just finished dropping his coloured balls and Jammy had forgotten to turn up altogether. Benny told me his albino rats didn't need to rehearse and that was the last I saw of him till Saturday. Chico pulled up a table and then put the three little plastic cups down.

'Have I ever shown you this delightful trick what my dear old dad once taught me?' he began chirpily.

'Loads of times,' I muttered, feeling properly fed up. 'And your dear old dad used to do it round all the fair-grounds in London.'

Anyway, he tried it out on me and I got it right by some miracle and he pretended to faint on the floor. I lifted the cup and there indeed was the little white ball.

'Needs practice,' I advised him. He opened one eye but stayed on the drama hall carpet.

In case you're wondering what I meant when I told Sandy that the problem of the police was being seen to, this was the first time Murphy lent us a helping hand. I'm not sure why; just the thought of scoring one over the Old Bill, I suppose – his second worst enemy.

Anyway, the Police Station was right at the end of the Market Square and nicely tucked away out of sight, over-looking the fields, the Berkeley road and the castle en-trance, but not much else. So Murphy happened to come pedalling merrily along on Saturday morning at half-past ten when a Ford Cortina, driven by Chico's brother Dean, approaches in the opposite direction. A screech of brakes, girls and old ladies and oh dear, it looks like something terrible has come to pass right outside the Old Billery. Has Murph been run over? He is lying across the road causing a traffic jam already. But here comes PC Blackwood, the burly father of Wendy Backbender, to restore order. He checks if the unconscious cyclist is dead or alive and if the yobby motorist is under the influence or not.

It took them ages to sort out the whole thing before discovering that nobody was hurt, or hit and that Murph had fallen off his bike from sheer fright and Dean had stopped his car just in time.

Meanwhile, further up the road the show had got started. The secret of Street Theatre is not so much the timing of it but finding the right pitch. Davy, Donna and Vento the ventriloquist had parked their act outside the bank, thinking that was the best place for the rich and generous to gather.

Shane, the mighty Wonder-dog, was the star attraction beyond a doubt and after I'd banged the music department's drum and shouted, 'Roll up! Roll up! Roll up to see Shane, the amazing acrobatic dog who will perform all his stunts without a net; Cola, the incredible juggling boy-wonder and Vento, a ventriloquist with not one, but two unbelievably life-like dummies . . .' the Swanswell Street Theatre began.

Shane, being a right show-off, gave an excited yelp and stood on his hind legs and pranced about a bit, finally heading a ball into the five people watching. That was all he did. But Donna's doll-face and baby blue eyes had the small crowd eating out of her hand. Davy, alias Cola in clown make-up, threw his first ball up too high and lost his rhythm straight away. Shane the Wonder-dog, seeing another colourful ball bouncing around, came racing in on the act and with a great leap caught the ball in his jaws in mid-air. He also knocked Davy off his feet.

'Flaming hell, Shane,' cussed Cola quietly. 'Stop trying

to steal my limelight.' The crowd, however, thought this was all part of the act and laughed and clapped heartily.

I then pulled my chair up with Beryl on one knee and Cheryl on the other, (superb dummies if not very convincing girls), and the Great Vento started up his act. 'Hello ladies and gentlemen – I am Vento and these two girls are called Cheese and Pickles and they are both madly in love with me. I do not know which one I fancy the most – I shall have to ask them both a question and see which of them is the most clever . . . ahem. . . .'

I had to give Beryl, or Cheryl, a shake because she was staring round the square with her finger in her mouth. It wasn't real ventriloquism, I confess, because they did the speaking while I pretended to throw my voice. Behind their doll masks you couldn't really see that their lips were moving normally – except when they stuck their stupid fingers in their mouths!

'Now then, tell me, Cheese, what is the difference between a fisherman and a lazy schoolboy. . . ?' Not the funniest joke ever heard, but it was all I could find in my old book of *A Thousand Golden Gags*.

I could hear a quiet whirring sound coming from her head as she thought hard, then: 'I knows . . . one baits his book . . . and the other hates his hook!' Beryl, or Cheryl, shrieked nice and loud and back to front.

'Wrong way round!' I hissed out of the corner of the clown's white mouth. Does she repeat it correctly? No, she starts to giggle. So there I sit with a speechless dummy on my knee all shivering with giggles.

'Right . . . er, Pickles, now it is your turn, seeing as your sister's such an idiot – now tell me, Pickles; how do you get four elephants into a mini?'

'That's easy!' she shrieks, twice as loud as her sister, who is still giggling, now behind her hand. 'Four in the front and four in the back!'

Then she realised she'd said it wrong as well and she started to giggle. 'He must be a good ventriloquist,' called out someone's dad in a loud sarcastic voice. 'He can giggle and tell bloody silly jokes at the same time. . . .'

He got a bigger laugh than I did. Thankfully he went off to do some shopping and took his wide-eyed son with him, reducing the seething masses to four people.

'Come on, Ducker, get off and let's see Davy's dog again,' shouted Benny's fat, white-haired gran. Suddenly feeling very annoyed and sheepish, I shook the two dummies on to the pavement and left Donna playing a pathetic tune on her recorder, while the crowd grew larger and laughed at the acrobatic antics of Shane the Wonder-dog and family.

Every time I held the drum out for money there was the same reaction: 'Ooh lovely, collecting for charity are you?' Purses and handbags click open. 'Who says kids these days cause nothing but trouble?' Hands delve into the wealth. 'Which charity did you say it was, dearie?' Swanswell Swimming Pool Appeal? Purses and bags click shut; faces go all squashed and red. 'Not you lot again! I don't know what that Headmaster thinks he's doing! Kids these days – nothing but trouble-makers!!'

As I crossed the square I noticed Benny's albino rats were collecting quite a crowd outside Streeter's. All the rats did was run up his arms, over his shoulders and then one of them, Pinky or Billy, would sit on his head and gaze thoughtfully at the rabble.

'Put 'ee down yer trousers, Ben!' shouted a gorilla from Arnold's Grill.

'You wouldn't do that, would yuh, Ben,' his chimp friend shouted next. 'The smell 'ud kill 'un!'

The two fell about laughing, but luckily Ben's bigger, much bigger brother was lurking around protectively and soon they were back inside the Grill feeding on bananas safely.

Watching and waiting his turn was Chico with his table. After a patter of applause he stepped forward. 'Very good, Ben, gerroff and make way for the star. Now then, lays and germs, cast your kindly eyes on this table before you and you'll see that the white ball is under the green cup so I move the cups around and the little white ball is under the red cup. . . .'

And off he went at four hundred miles an hour, only this time there was no mistake. After I had collected the few measly pence that Benny had raised and put it on the drum letting Chico collect his own fee separately – it was part of the deal – I saw that Jammy had at last decided to turn up; thirty minutes late.

I positioned the sleepy musician on the dosser's bench under the town hall clock where everyone would be sure to see and hear him. He was the last act left.

Talk about last but not least. He was even better than I had hoped. He must have practised it for us. He could play anthing – a bit of classical stuff: the tune out of Mozart's *Night Music*; some Bach, then into the serious stuff, like *Evita* and *Cats* and so on. It was great the way the shoppers, even those who weren't watching the Street Theatre, seemed to stop in their tracks to listen and then look round wondering where the beautiful noise was coming from. And they were so grateful to him for brightening up their lives a little they were even prepared to fork our more than 10p at a time.

It was as if the sun had come out and the buildings round the square were gleaming clean and white under clear blue skies; as if the snarl and growl of the traffic was part of his orchestral accompaniment. And everybody started smiling.

He was half-way through something called 'Mountains of Mourne' when this huge, red-faced gingery bloke came striding towards the bench mopping his face with a spotted red handkerchief. He was streaming tears.

'That's beautiful, me boy, ah beautiful to be sure,' he moaned in an Irish ecstasy that had everybody backing away. He pulled the startled Jammy by the arm till he'd swayed him off the bench. 'Don't be wasting yer fiddle out here, me boy! That song is wasted on these people – come along, come along now, come along here and play that to me mates and there you'll be well and truly appreciated. . . .'

It was Murphy's Uncle Joxer who'd crossed the water for his summer holidays. He hauled Jammy round the corner to the den of vice and iniquity, 'The Buglehorn', where Murph's mother was barmaid. Outside the pub door Uncle Joxer was bending his knees, peering into Jammy's face like it was a coal cellar and asking him if he knew this dance or that jig. Each time he asked, Jammy shook his head and glanced uneasily round for help. In the end Joxer said: 'Ah never mind, never mind, we'll be teaching you the tunes, so we will. . . .'

And he disappeared into the gloomy bar dragging the panic-stricken genius behind him.

The sound of yelps and shrieks had me back at the bench wondering where the commotion was coming from. The other side of the road featured Donna Dollface shrieking and shouting some very rude words after a pack of scruffy dogs, some trailing leads, some trailing owners, who were all chasing after Shane the amazing acrobatic dog. Past the bank they raced, past the antique shop, on past the police station and into PC Blackwood, who was still trying to make sense of Murphy's story after all this time.

I wondered for a horrible moment if Shane and Co were going to divert PC Blackwood's attention from our diversion. Behind me, as I watched the hunt end in a pile of dogs, bodies, bikes and police helmet, the halting, high-pitched sounds of Jammy's violin began to pick out the tune of an Irish jig. To cheers and shouts the tune was completed, repeated and repeated more fluently and much quicker.

I had to have a quick peek at Jammy's Jig and there he was, on the table with the blokes clapping, jigging from one foot to the other, twirling each other round and generally having the time of their lives. Then it all came to a halt with a crash of chairs, tables and bottles and a roar of applause and he was picking out the tune of yet another jig. 'Can you play this one; it goes dee-diddly-ay, diddly-ay, diddly-dee-dee?'

'Scram, Ducker! It's the Fuzz! We been busted!' shouted a warning voice and I saw Murphy standing on his pedals, cycling like fury out of the square. Dean's beat-up Cortina pulled up by the kerb and he asked me, elbow on window ledge if I'd seen his kid brother. I hadn't. I looked round at the remnants of the Street Theatre. Benny was still entertaining the crowds with his albino rats, but Chico, jealous of the competition perhaps, was nowhere to be seen. PC Blackwood was though.

His red face, bearded and bristling with rage was glowering in his blue uniform like a gathering storm as he came marching down the pavement towards the town hall. Leaving the sounds of Jammy's Jig dancing round the pub, I ran across the road ready to take refuge in Streeters.

I jumped out the way just in time as Mr Pegson came roaring out of the shop doorway. 'Nearly got you there, young 'un!' he shouted cheerfully and tooted his horn. Don't ask me how he recognised me in all the make-up, but funnily most people did.

'Be getting the new one soon,' he told me proudly. 'It goes up and down kerbs and is twice as fast as this one.'

'Great!' I muttered, wondering why he was so keen to tell me all this.

'Cost me a packet too,' he continued nodding and waiting. In the end he had to tell me himself. 'Not that I can't afford it . . . not now that is.'

'B-but I thought they cost nearly a thousand pounds,' I stammered.

'They do, and thanks to you and young Coley I can afford it,' he informed me mysteriously. I gaped. He beamed back at me. 'That picture you found? The one you thought was a Constable and bought off me to sell at the antique shop? T'was a Cotman. The water-colour man; one of the great genii of the English Landscape, they say. I knew I'd heard his name somewhere. On the Open University – Art Foundation Course, unit three. Cotman. That picture's a minor masterpiece, so they tell me in Bristol. I goes and buys it back off the antique shop for a fiver, then me nephew takes us down to the Bristol art gallery and they say it's worth two or three thousand pound. You're never too old to strike lucky, eh young 'un? Never too old to learn neither. . . .'

And leaving me to disappear in a crack in the wall he tooted his horn, raised his hat and was off roaring down the pavement of the High Street, scattering shoppers, dogs and police.

Benny, still blissfully juggling rats, hadn't noticed the blue uniformed trouble-maker heading his way. I raced across to tell him, still holding my snare-drum as Blackwood paused to peer at me thoughtfully. 'Where did Chico get to?' I asked after I'd tipped him off. Benny put the rats back in their box, much to the disappointment of the crowd. Then he lifted his mask up.

'He went off with a Japanese tourist to the castle,' he told me.

I looked round quickly for the table of tricks but couldn't see it. Don't tell me he was doing his 'Where's the Ball' to a coachload of Japanese. It could cause an international outrage.

Then there was a heavy hand on my shoulder. 'Supposing you tell me what's going on around here, whoever you are under that stupid make-up.' It was PC Blackwood booming down at me.

'Er . . . it's oi, innit, Clark Burroughs,' I told him. He seemed satisfied. 'We ain't doin' nothin' . . . much!'

'Oh no – what *are* you doing, Burroughs, tell me that?'

Imitating Clark Burroughs must have cramped my style a bit because I couldn't think of a clever answer. And the longer he waited, hands on hips, peering down into my face the greater the chance of his eventually recognising me.

It was a disturbance behind him that made him straighten up and turn round. A bottle had come crashing through one of the windows of 'The Buglehorn' and even from here it sounded like one almighty punch-up was going on inside.

'It do look like trouble,' I said, to get him to hurry up and leave me alone. He stroked his thick beard thoughtfully; very thoughtfully. 'It sounds like the Irish in "The Buglehorn",' he announced and continued to stroke his beard. To my relief he began to move away, taking the smallest steps possible for such large, flat feet and proceeded to proceed in a north-westerly direction down the market square. To my greater relief I saw Jammy come staggering out of the pub clutching his violin and with his mask on. Seeing the mask, PC Blackwood connected him with me and span round.

'Burroughs!' he shouted and pointed his finger. 'He's one of your lot!'

'So? Ta-ta, slob!' I chirped cheekily and raced off down the road to the castle.

As I ambled wearily through the gates and into the car-park, I saw a coach and a fair-sized crowd huddling round its rear. There, surrounded by about two dozen Japanese was Chico. A man with glasses and moustache had just handed him a shiny, golden quid and Chico was off: 'Ah so banzai – torah-torah – now you see ball is under the gleen cup so I move gleen cup and led cup and so ball must be under little brue cup, ah so. . . .'

Even with the silly accent the patter was wasted, but they were at least watching the ball and cup very closely. Chico finished; the man pointed to the red cup. Chico pretended to peek under it then lifted it clear off the table. There was a loud gasping groan and the whole group started criticising each other. One person at the end, who I supposed was the tour operator or guide, was getting very annoyed with all this and kept trying to persuade them back to the coach. But they had lost interest in Ye Olde Englande for a time, preferring instead the New Generation.

'How is honourable Paul Daniels getting on?' I asked out the corner of my mouth. Before he could reply, the tourists, seeing the two of us there in make-up, insisted on taking a photo. The two clowns posed before two dozen Japanese cameras. They probably thought we were a nation of clowns and con-men anyway.

'You wouldn't believe it,' he replied from under his make-up. 'You would not believe how much I'm making with this lot.'

'Well watch it, PC Blackwood's on the prowl,' I warned him, thinking he'd done enough business for that day. Chico swallowed heavily and started to pack up.

'Oh so solly,' he said and bowed. They all smiled and bowed. Such polite people the Japanese. 'So solly, Suzuki and Kawasaki. Please forgive, am Honda way home.'

He pointed to the entrance and passed his finger across his throat. 'Old Billo, Harry Kiri, and Kamikaze!'

But as we headed out of the castle grounds he would not be specific about the amount of loot he'd raised. He'd tell me on Monday, having deducted the cricket match winnings, no doubt. Dean caught up with us almost immediately after that and dropped me off at the school.

Then I returned the drum and along with the others removed my make up.

'How did it go?' asked Sandy uneasily. I gave him the round O sign.

'Davy said you had a bit of trouble,' he noted. I glanced round. No sign of Davy. No sign of Jammy either.

'Trouble?' I scoffed. 'The Swimming Pool Appeal cause trouble? Please!'

16. Many Happy Returns

*'Orally proficient, but shows greater ingenuity in
his excuses than in his approach to the subject'*
French, Miss Pyatt

Needless to say, yet again I kept a very low profile when I
got back. I whistled a lot and smiled at everybody and
made sure neither Mum nor Dad went near a radio at one
o'clock in case our Street Theatre was on the news. I offered
to wash up the lunch dishes and saucepans and soon I was
scalding my fingers in a soapy maelstrom. Mum and Dad
went to Dursley to do some quick shopping, probably to see
if there were any handcuffs or balls-and-chains going
cheap.

Half-way up the middle prong of a dirty fork I felt this
tug at my sleeve. I turned round and there staring up at me
like a ghost was the blond-haired, white-faced Spencer
Burroughs. Again.

'What the hell are you doing here now?' I shrieked, and
yes, the kitchen door was half open again. Time we kept it
locked, I realised.

'I did wonder if you did have any jobs to do?' he announced and noticed me looking over his head. 'The others
have gone to the canal, so it's all right.'

'Jobs? You mean you want to help raise money for the
appeal?' I checked. He didn't move. Then I had an idea.
Not a stroke of genius, but an idea. I got our red plastic
bucket from under the sink and started to fill it with water.
How would he like to go round the neighbourhood washing
cars? He didn't seem worried either way and stared into the
bucket of soapy water when I presented it to him. I'd
forgotten a chamois.

'A quid each car and ten for a Rolls,' I joked, steering him through the doorway. And off he went like a little blond robot. He homed in on the Skinners' dusty blue Metro, which badly needed a good scrubbing and hoped that was the last I'd seen of him for the rest of the day. I left him throwing soapy sledges over the blue roof. He didn't smile once but the way he was rocking the car about with his scrubbing and rubbing looked like real eagerness to me.

I set the stump up in the back garden. After all, the County trials were less than two weeks away. Summer traffic zoomed past our hedge: cyclists. 'Wayee, Ducker!' Some from school, some red-faced strangers on tour. A squadron of Mods on scooters roared past, tank aerials waving in the wind. An occasional caravan. It was a gorgeous afternoon with the sky a soft blue blanket of gentle warmth stretched over everyone.

Suddenly a cropped pink head with earrings appeared at the hedge. 'Hey you! Botham-head!' Baz called to me as my out-swinger missed the stump by fractions of a mile. 'What time does this spit and saw-dust joint open then?'

'Six o'clock, sir,' I told him, sounding like Dad. He was all hot and beaded with sweat, stripped to the waist, wearing a green and red head-band. He had 'Madness' tattooed on his chest. Fair comment.

'Flipping six o'clock?' he roared, swinging his helmet irritably. His skinny co-pilot took her helmet off and rolled her eyes in disgust. She was about sixteen and swung this posh-looking camera over her shoulder. Hanging on to his sweaty carcass must have been like trying to grab a bar of soap in the bath. 'Right then, darling, Arnold's Grill it is!'

He replaced the black helmet on his pink helmet, rolled his motorised hair-drier on to the road, popped, lurched and roared off down the hill to the railway bridge.

As I went to retrieve the ball, another sweaty head appeared over the hedge. This time it was the little car-cleaner robot. He looked very agitated too. Must have needed re-programming.

'D-Ducker?' he called. He was trembling. 'I – I'm in trouble. Honest.'

Well, if he was honest, how could he be in trouble? He trotted round the hedge and we met in the car-park driveway.

'I was cleaning the car,' he explained. 'And there was this camera in the back seat, right?'

'And you picked it up to look at it and dropped it, right?' I guessed gloomily.

'Nooh! It ain't there no more. Somebody must have come along and nicked it. But when old Skinner finds out he'll think it was me.'

To my horror he started to cry. 'You got to help me, Ducker. They'll send me to Borstal, honest. Then I'll never get to Africa.'

Great streams went gushing down his cheeks. I sort of half put my arm round him. 'All right, all right. Take it easy. Of course I'll help you. I haven't paid you back for returning the raffle money yet. Don't worry. With Ducker here you're in the clear. I'll get the camera back. . . .'

God knows how. But I felt really sorry for young Spence. Miss Bleach was right. They were always number one suspect. It's a crime to accuse people without any proof!

But I had to hurry; the car was almost cleaned and Skinner was about to come out and check any minute. I calmed Spence down long enough to get the story clear. Skinner had carelessly left his camera on the edge of the back seat. Some little kids on bikes had stopped to tease Spence. Could have been them. A skinhead on a scooter stopped to ask him where the best pub was. And the girl had a camera slung over her shoulder, I remembered. Why wasn't it round her neck? Either she'd been taking pictures, or it had just been handed to her by her thieving, thuggish boyfriend, who, even now, was treating her to coke and crisps in Arnold's Grill. This was a job for Ducker the Wonderboy. With a pat on Spencer's head I rushed off to get my trusty bike.

Soon I was pedalling helter-skelter into Berkeley, and with every revolution of the pedals I asked myself how the hell I was going to get the camera back once I'd arrived.

I parked my bike round the corner, strolled along the pavement, turned up my shirt collars, put on my toughest face and trotted up the steps. Then I stumbled blindly into the dark world of Arnold's Grill.

Despite being a lovely day outside it was packed; and nearly all of the clientele were scooter riders. I even recognised a few. For a moment I felt like turning round and slinking out. Through the blue fog the juke box hammered at the walls and screamed at us to 'Run for the Hills'. Good idea. Against the opposite wall was a cluster of coloured lights and bleeping noises that took money off people foolish enough to try their luck. Suddenly there was an explosion of coins, bleeps and metallic gurgles as a lucky winner went wild over the jackpot.

I strode meekly up to the counter for a coke and Oxo crisps. They only had plain left. A voice tutted loudly in my left ear.

'Put your money away, Ducker – this one's on me!' It was Chico with his tall, dark brother Dean. Chico had been the lucky winner. We found a half-empty table and ignored the two leather-clad bikers as best we could.

'This is my lucky day, Ducker,' he told me cheerfully, while I sat watching Baz and his mates at the opposite tables. The camera was next to the sauce bottle. Chico span a coin in the air. 'What with the Japs this morning and the jackpot just now nothing can go wrong. . . .'

He noticed my anxious glances. 'That is unless you're going to bring me bad luck, Ducker. What exactly are you doing here?'

As I told him, his smile disappeared slowly. He understood. 'I see; you're going to nick back this camera to save your little mate Spencer Burroughs from getting into trouble? Very noble. How?'

'I'm glad you asked me that, Chico, because I thought, if, er . . . you were . . . to create a diversion, you know, cause a disturbance, I. . . .'

'Me, cause a disturbance in here, for you? Cheerio, Ducker!'

'Listen, if you could distract them, just for a few seconds. . . .'

'No chance. Have a nice day. . . .'

'All right then; if I cause a disturbance and you. . . .'

'I reckon we caused enough disturbances for you,' grunted Dean sourly and frowned at me through a perfect smoke ring. 'Your best bet is to beat it!'

'Hang on,' said Chico after a pause, sitting up slowly and staring across at the scooter gang. 'Do you see what I see?'

I turned in my chair and looked. There, right next to the camera and under Baz's tattooed forearm, was the Sharp ghetto blaster. Chico stood up and motioned me to my feet. 'I'll cause the disturbance, and you can nick them both.'

I nodded nervously. He told me to lurk at the back until it was time. I lurked, saw Chico go and buy himself a burger and chips, sit down, sniff it, get up, take it back to the counter, get cussed, return to his table, sit down, sniff it and start eating. With only one chip left on his plate he rose in his chair, clutching his stomach, spitting out bits of gristle, a look of perfect agony on his face. Then with a loud, strangled shout of 'NO!' he slid slowly to the floor. Everybody jumped to their feet and crowded round. Seconds later I was tiptoeing down the steps with a ghetto blaster under my arm and the camera round my neck.

Cycling with all that clobber was not easy and just as I wobbled down the High Street they all came piling down the steps shouting 'Stop thief!' and worse. Unfortunately they spotted me as I was turning the corner at the bottom of the hill into Jumper's Lane. I pedalled unsteadily along by the river, certain I could hear the wasp-drone of scooters in the distance. I passed the caravan park and then swung right, hoping they'd go zooming straight on to the power station.

For a time it looked as though I'd lost them all and when I arrived, breathless, back at the Skinners' house Spencer was still cleaning the car while a puzzled and slightly irritated Mr Skinner stood watching him with his hands on his hips. How was I going to sneak the camera into the back seat without his seeing?

'Don't you think you cleaned it enough?' he was saying as Spencer rubbed stubbornly away at the windscreen. He looked up at me plaintively. I tried to get rid of Skinner.

'Isn't that your phone ringing, Mr Skinner?' He listened, shook his head, and started to walk round the car. As long as he didn't look inside.

'Hey!' he shouted, looking inside. 'Hey you! Have you seen my camera?'

Pushing Spencer aside he wrenched the door open and rummaged about in the back seat while I held the camera behind my back.

'Sorry about that,' Skinner chuckled after he'd stood up, opened the case and stroked his expensive camera lovingly. 'Thought you'd nicked it for a moment.' He looked at Spencer thoughtfully. 'It tipped off the edge of the seat on to the floor. You must have been rocking the car a bit.'

Spencer sort of crouched away in blank terror as Mr Skinner checked that his camera was all right. I crouched in blank terror now wondering what the hell to do with the camera I'd just stolen; thanks to that stupid, little albino gorilla.

Without another word I got back on my bike, still

holding the ghetto blaster, and raced off one more time, thinking of leaving it at the police station, pretending to have found it, somewhere. But as I was passing the pub a red Ford Cortina heading in the opposite direction screeched to a halt and a door swung open.

'Ducker!' shouted Chico as I screeched to a halt as well. He ran over to me. 'Ducker, you've got two minutes to tell me what the hell's going on before Baz and his gang realise you've given them the slip and come back from the power station. Starting now!'

I handed him the camera. He frowned down at it. 'Now what?' 'You can handle it, Chico,' I flattered him in desperation. 'Tell them anything you like. Say it was a mistake, say you nicked it back off me, say you had to kill me for it. . . .'

'I won't tell them that,' Chico interrupted morally. 'Baz would really be annoyed. He's going to kill you himself, slowly.'

I shuddered, then remembered something else. I ran across to the pub, raced upstairs, took the polythene bag of loot from my desk drawer, raced down and handed it over.

'The raffle money?' he squawked doubtfully. 'Where did you get from?'

'You'd never believe it if I told you; but think about it,' I urged now, really worried. 'You return the camera to the crumpet on the scooter; you give the gang their money back and sort out the whole mess single-handed. You'll keep your ghetto blaster, and they'll think you're brilliant.'

'They know that already,' he answered with slow, thoughtful modesty. 'But that poor doll was really upset you nicked her expensive camera. Yeah, when I hand it back personally, she'll be very impressed. Yeah, I like the idea. . . .'

He went all dreamy-eyed for a moment until Dean blew the horn. Chico jumped back. 'By the way,' he added and poked my chest pocket, 'the flipping batteries are flat. They've been playing my ghetto blaster day and flipping night. That's half a dozen Duracell you owe me.'

There's gratitude for you. But off he went to intercept the scooters, taking my one remaining headache with me. Or rather last but one, for as I turned to go back into the pub to lie down for a few days, I nearly trampled over Spencer Burroughs and his little red bucket. He peered up into my face cautiously.

'All right now, is it?' he ventured. Then he dug deep into his jeans. 'Oh and here's the quid.' He handed me a shiny, golden quid. 'For the whatsit.'

I handed it back. He didn't want to take it at first, to my surprise, but I insisted. I was so relieved in the end that we'd managed to avoid disaster. 'And we'll call you if, er . . . if we need any more jobs doing,' I said. He nearly smiled. Glad to feel wanted I suppose.

I wandered uneasily into the kitchen. Spencer was saved from Borstal, or whatever; Chico had his cassette player back. (He got banned from Arnold's Grill though.) The scooter gang had their raffle money back and I was still alive – for the time being. I prayed quietly that Chico had managed to talk Baz and his gang out of any murderous intentions. Or perhaps he'd distracted him by chatting up his girl-friend.

In the distance I seemed to hear a scooter droning nearer. I locked the kitchen door and hid under the table, and stayed under the table long after it had passed. The sound of a scooter still makes my blood run cold.

17. Jackpot! (At last)

'Shows great appreciation and understanding of the past, but I would appreciate it if he were less of a nuisance in the future'   Humanities, Mr K. Sutherland

Sunday morning I breezed over to Ruthie's to find out how her dog-jog had got on. She didn't sound very enthusiastic so it must have been a disaster.

'What was all that trouble in the square on Saturday?' she asked me.

'Trouble? What do I know of trouble? Must have been the Burroughs gang!'

Then it was over to Jammy's. He lived in an old house at the edge of the common. I rang his bell and his large mother opened it.

'Oh! Oh . . . it's you,' she repeated, scowling down at me. Reluctantly she let me in as I explained that I'd brought some notes for her son.

'But I thought you and Julian had been split up,' she remembered, which caused a slight inconvenience.

'Er . . . yes, but we do the same work in humanities, and as his teacher ran out of her lesson last week. . . .'

'Ran out of the lesson?' she rumbled in disbelief.

'Miss Bleach was having another of her emotional crises,' I went on.

'Emotional crises?' Mrs Armstrong-Mayes gaped and put her horn-rimmed glasses on. She usually carried these on a chain dangling on her mountainous bosom. 'What on earth goes on at that school?'

'It's 3F you see,' I said, stirring it nicely. 'They're a real shower. They say the teachers draw lots to see who has them. . . .'

Without answering, she wandered vaguely back to her study. Then something clicked and she turned. 'I don't suppose you know where he went yesterday?' she asked. I lied whitely. 'He came home giggling to himself like a lunatic – in fact he was giggling all afternoon – his father is convinced he'd been sniffing glue.'

And she disappeared behind the study door and busied herself with some typing. She could type really fast too. It sounded like a chariot race in there.

Jammy was practising his scales when I got upstairs ready to take the money off him. He was still smiling to himself.

'By the way, how much did you make?' he asked, jauntily swinging his violin by the neck. I squirmed with embarrassment. When I said 70p he did his glue-sniffing act for me.

'Wasn't my fault!' I defended. 'Those two dummies Beryl and Cheryl kept saying the punch-lines back to front. And you?'

He was already counting out the golden quids, Wellingtons and Florence Nightingales for me.

'Fifty quid?' I gasped. I knew he was good, but this made him worth his weight in gold.

'It's the Irish,' he explained coolly. 'They're the only ones who appreciate talent, artistry and genius. Here, Ducker, what d'you think of this?'

And swinging his violin up under his chin he played an Irish jig at twice the speed of dancing. Before I could stop him to ask what the punch-up was about, he was playing number two and number three. 'This last one's my favourite, "The Siege of Ennis",' he said as I gave up and sat on a stool listening. He was so naturally brilliant I didn't even feel jealous, much. He paused and sighed sadly.

'It was after that they started their punch-up – they all had this big argument about which one to play next. First it

157

was who paid me the most, then they decided to fight each other for it. Before I knew what was happening it was like a humanities lesson.'

This time we both giggled. At least the Irish were generous before they started wrecking the place. And he had to go and play to them next Saturday. It's not always handy being a genius.

'I still think it was jolly tight splitting us up,' he confessed as we sat remembering the bad old days. 'Why didn't they put Chico Marks in 3F?'

'That would have been a brain-wave,' I scoffed contemptuously. 'You and me in 3L and Chico with Burroughs in 3F? It would have been twice as bad.'

'Chico doesn't go around with Burroughs,' he pointed out. 'Never did. He's not in the same league. Burroughs is just a moron.'

'He's got no sense of humour either,' I added. I then told him about Chico and the Japanese tourists forking out a shiny, golden quid to try and spot the ball. Come to think of it, he must have made quite a packet too. 'Being such an expert on Irish jigs now, do you know "Old Mother Riley's Pram"?' I asked just before I left with his little bag of loot. He shook his head but seemed eager to learn yet another tune.

'No I don't – how does it go?'

'You push it!' And hooting with laughter I thundered down the stairs.

'Not surprised you only made 70p,' he called down after me, 'telling crappy jokes like that.' And he played the first bars of 'Colonel Bogey' to speed my exit.

I was right about Chico though, on both counts. We were all in the pottery room celebrating. Room Two was too risky these days.

'Wait for it, lads.' Chico held us in suspense, then produced a roll of money. He counted it out, licking his fingers now and then, as we licked our lips. When he passed fifty Jammy swallowed hard. When he passed sixty we all swallowed hard.

'My God!' I murmured.

'No, Ducker – mine!' Chico quipped, kissing the loot.

'How the hell did you manage to raise sixty-three quid?' Jammy asked, shaking his head in disbelief.

'Genius, Julian old chum, merely genius,' he explained modestly and combed his hair twice.

'That makes one hundred and twenty altogether,' I calculated. 'And we've passed five hundred at last.'

Jammy nodded sourly, then pointed out something that had been on everybody's mind. 'Of course, if we raise nine hundred and ninety nine pounds ninety pence,' he began slowly as the others looked up, 'and Ruthie's little gang raise a thousand first, we have to add ours to theirs – right, Ducker?' I didn't say anything. They all knew the answer anyway. 'If that does happen, Ducker, I shall have to invite my Irish mates along to your pub every night.'

'Yeah,' sneered Chico in agreement. 'Daft innit? Just 'cos loverboy's playing hard to get with frustrated vicar's daughter.'

'Be a sport, Ducker,' crooned Jammy. 'Try and be nice to her till the end of term. Think of the money, that's all. . . .'

I ignored this tedious teasing and noticed Noddy Bright racing round the car-park like a lunatic looking for something. Seeing me, he pointed his finger at me and came running up the steps, trailing a crowd of curious first and second years. He was always showing his 'C' scope off to the little 'uns.

'You all laughed at me!' he shouted and tugged a piece of paper out of his jacket pocket. 'You all laughed at my treasure-hunting! Well go and read that, go on!'

Poor Noddy, I had no idea what had got into him; he was almost hysterical. Perhaps his dad had been belting him too hard lately. Jammy took the piece of paper and unfolded it dubiously. It was a letter from the museum in Bristol.

'I took them my treasure, didn't I? Like you said,' he shouted, even louder so that kids were peering round the corner from the art room. 'And when they did see it –' Then he actually stood on a chair. 'They did say it's worth thousands of pounds.'

'Oh yeah,' Davy laughed glancing at Jammy. Of course everything Noddy found was worth tens of thousands at least. I waited for Jammy to finish reading the famous letter.

'Hang on, you lot,' he waved us into instant silence. The paper trembled. '"Dear Nigel, We have now examined your findings and are pleased to tell you that they are both ancient and probably of . . . great value . . . – the sword could be at least a thousand years old. . . ."'

Noddy, still standing on his chair, was nodding down at us. Jammy continued: '"We would like to explore the area further . . . etc . . . etc. As to your enquiry into the exact value of the sword and brooch, we can't say precisely at this stage but it is probably valued in the region of . . ."' he looked over the top of the shaking paper at us, sort of frowning, finding the words difficult to pronounce . . . '"in the region of several thousand pounds!"'

In stunned silence they all looked up at their saviour; their money-maker supreme; their treasure-seeker extraordinary; the Genius. I always knew he'd strike lucky one day – when he was the same age as old man Pegson! The pottery room erupted. Noddy was pulled off his chair, patted to death and surrounded by whooping, cheering congratulations. I must admit, I hung back at first. There had to be something wrong somewhere. Everything else we thought was good money had been a dangled cherry whipped away at the moment of biting. Knowing Noddy, they'd got his junk mixed up with somebody else with the same name. And if it was real treasure, what about Farmer Gilpin who owned the land? He'd want a share of it too.

The rest of them had no such doubts. We'd done it. He'd done it. Once he'd made up the thousand he could keep the change, they decided. And that meant we would all have the pleasure of seeing Ruthie Pendryll handing her paltry sum over to us. That I couldn't wait to see.

Everybody raced off to the tuck-shop to buy him coke, coke, coke and crisps. It was a bemused and quietly belching Noddy who was led back into Room Two at the end of break. Ruthie too looked bemused when I said, 'By the way – how much are you contributing towards the pool?'

She didn't answer but frowned uneasily. I had the letter from the museum now and unfolded it as I explained. 'You did say the first to reach a thousand?'

She nodded. 'So come on then, how much did you make?' She was trying to see what the posh-looking letter said.

'We've made five hundred and eighty pounds so far – why?' I waited for her to ask me how much we'd managed but she wouldn't play. So I just gave her the letter and let her read.

We saw her face go white, eyes standing out on stalks, saw her lips mouth the magic words, 'thousands of pounds'. But typical Ruthie she has to go and read the rest of the letter, right through to the 'yours sincerely'.

Instead of fainting or surrendering, she folded up the paper and gave it back. 'Well?' she asked emptily. Well? Is that all she can say in the face of defeat? 'Where are these thousands of pounds? I can't see them. Can you? It's all very well bringing me little letters with the words "thousands of pounds" but unless you can count it out on to a table in front of me . . . it doesn't count at all.'

And raising her chin at us, she grabbed her bag and stalked out to the next lesson. This was playing dirty, I reckoned, not that telling her would have made any difference. So I sat next to Noddy to make sure it really was all in the bag.

We exchanged notes and it did look safe and sound. There would be some delay because of something called 'Treasure Trove' and they had to inform the coroner. Once they'd got his permission, the museum would pay Noddy the full value of the treasure. It was too good to be true. Everybody would be happy: the museum gets the sword and brooch; he has his money; we have the difference; and Ruthie at last has to eat humble pie, in public!

Mind you, I didn't like the note which said 'A week, maybe two or longer!' That meant we could be sitting around for days doing nothing but basking in glory watching Ruthie gradually reaching her goal and come marching back to us on July the 17th with her hand held open.

Dinner break and I was in the office handing over the money to Mrs Franklin to put in the safe. Des Grisewald and some girls were just behind me, presumably about to do the same. The two little piles would then rest innocently side-by-side.

'Money?' Mrs F. said in surprise, glowering at both our parties. 'I thought Mr Thorne had forbidden any fund-raising.'

'That was only in school miss,' I explained politely. Des oozed forward. 'That's OK Janet I'll take it,' and lifting the bag out of my hand he took the keys off the hook on the wall and sloped off into the store room.

Thornie himself appeared in the doorway, looking grey and worn and haggard, as usual. I was hoping he wouldn't, but he did – he beckoned me outside, down the gloomy corridor and into his office. I didn't sit down, nor did he.

'Saturday morning,' he grunted, having been told at last. That was all he said, then he shuffled some papers together, waiting.

'Oh yes . . . er, Saturday . . .' I had grown tired of lying, so I told the truth as coolly as possible. Deep breath and brace yourself time. 'I knew you said the appeal was to be postponed till the holidays, but the kids were so keen that we thought if we kept it going outside the school it wouldn't matter. . . .'

He held up his hand. 'Look, look, I'm not accusing you of amnesia, I am accusing you of downright disobedience!' And he reinforced the shout with a slam on the desk top so that the pens rattled and framed photographs trembled. So did I.

'We just don't like giving up, sir,' I said hopefully. He didn't look very impressed, but started to fiddle with cigarette papers and tobacco and rolled himself another lolly-stick.

'This is just a case of stupid male pride,' he corrected. 'You don't like the idea of losing to the girls, that's all.' He paused and lit his faglet. 'How much have you raised anyway?'

'Five hundred, sir, more or less,' I decided to keep the sword a secret, a sort of pleasant surprise.

'You must be neck and neck then,' he realised, still angry. 'Add both your totals together and what d'you get? One thousand pounds. Has it ever occurred to you that had you joined forces with Ruth you'd have the money by now, with probably far less trouble and everybody would be happy . . . even me.'

I shrugged sheepishly and nodded. 'So why the hell are you two turning it into a battle of the sexes?' No answer. 'Have you tried talking to her about it? Tried to find some sort of compromise? You have? So what happened?'

'Some women are very tricky,' I said. He stared out the window and could not help nodding.

'They certainly are,' he agreed grimly. Then he turned back to his desk, altered the angle of the framed photo slightly and sadly shook his head. 'No, that's not totally true! Some women are tricky – very tricky. Lethal even – and I hope you never find that out for yourself.'

'So do I, sir,' I hoped.

'No, Ducker, the majority are good, better, best and do a magnificent job.' He straightened up and pointed his faglet fingers at me like a crossbow. 'The whole point of co-education is to show the moronic, arrogant male that it's the female which is the superior sex. . . .'

'Superior?' I blurted out in horror.

'Yes, boy! The majority of them are just that. Superior. Why when it comes to strength, patience and courage – we are like puppies and pygmies in comparison.'

'If you say so, sir,' I said, wondering which of the two he chose to be.

'Ruth's a good girl. She tries too hard sometimes, but she's all right. God knows what you said, or did to her to make her hate you the way she does,' he meditated meaningfully.

'She doesn't hate me, sir,' I explained. 'She just wants me to be . . . the sort of bloke she wants me to be . . . a pygmy!'

'But Ducker you *are* a pygmy! A borderline pygmy!' He snorted and gazed at the picture of a kestrel hanging on the office wall. The kestrel was his own, the painting was Sandy's. Sunday afternoons you could see him fly the bird on Stinchcombe Hill. 'By the way,' he added. 'While I was chasing after Clark Burroughs yesterday I popped into their cottage and had a quick chat with Fabia.' He sucked on the glowing lollipop stick. 'Asked her how things were going. . . .'

He waited for me to say something but I stayed silent. 'It was chaos in there as usual, but then, Ducker, some people, grown-ups, find it more difficult than others, you understand; find it difficult to cope – with bills, kids, ordinary housekeeping. Anyway, I asked her if she wanted anything and she looked me in the eye and said, "Yes, Mr Thorne. I want the do-gooders to leave me alone and let me sort myself out." So that's what we shall do for the time being, don't you think?'

I shrugged. This was a really strange conversation. He continued. 'I doubt if she'll be there much longer. You can see she's had more than enough.'

Mind you, he used to spring these confessions on you unexpectedly. I remembered he took a humanities lesson once, when Sutherland was recovering from his nervous breakdown. All he did was tell us about a sack of dead chicks he'd got from a local farmer. He was going to feed them to the kestrel, but as he opened the sack, he thought he heard a faint 'cheep'. He said he spent a whole hour checking every chick to make sure it was dead. He gave us all the creeps that lesson.

'Has it ever occurred to you, Ducker, that the reason why there's so much evil in the world is because doing good is often so damn difficult?'

'Er . . . no sir.'

'Well, now you know,' he nodded grimly and stubbed out his crumpled faglet in a sea shell on his desk. 'So if you want to do something good, don't bother with charitable acts, just stick to charity instead for the time being. Give money, raise money and that'll do. . . .'

'Does that include swimming pools, sir?' I asked. He sort of jerked. Then swung round, blue eyes blazing.

'Ducker . . . get out of here, before I have you expelled!'

This must have been a put-up job because after he'd kicked me out and I wandered back into the foyer, who should be waiting for me, greatly concerned, but two of the Superior Sex.

'What did he want you for this time?' asked Ruthie guiltily. 'You're not in trouble again are you?'

'Trouble, me?' I laughed at the idea. 'No, Ruth, he merely thanked me for all the hard work I was putting in and wished me good luck with the rest of the enterprise.'

'I bet he did,' muttered Dawn in delicious disbelief.

'He is on their side though,' added Ruth sourly. 'He has been all along. . . .'

'Huh!' I grunted back and put my hands in my pockets, another thing they couldn't do. Superior Sex indeed. 'I don't think he knows whose side he's on. You know, girls, I worry about old Thornie sometimes. . . .'

18. The Nastiest of Video Nasties

'A cheerful, lively pupil – sometimes too lively. He is very creative, though not always in a positive way'
Art, S. Sanderson

Apart from me and my nagging doubts, others were not too happy with Noddy's success. Chico for one.

'He went and spoilt the fun, getting it all in one go,' he remarked in the youth centre.

'Especially doing it legal, decent and honest,' I put in. Murphy was lining up for a cannon off the top pocket.

'Which reminds me,' he reminded me, 'I want that twenty-five quid back. If it's against your principles, it ain't against mine.' He meant the cricket money.

'What twenty-five quid's that, Chico?' I said very loud so that everybody stopped to listen. He cringed quietly.

'The point is, I had this brilliant little wheeze for raising two hundred quid and now we don't need it, do we?' he stated coldly.

I leaned back for a moment and took a good hard look at him.

'Why have you been so dead keen to raise money for the school, Chico?'

'What sort of question's that?' he snapped uncomfortably, then giggled. 'This has all been a lesson for you, Ducker my old mate, the great lesson of life. That the easiest thing in the world is to get money out of people. . . .'

'Yeah, but all the bent ways have never paid off have they?' I pointed out. 'Except your ball and cup trick of course.'

'My ball and cup trick was not bent!' he shouted angrily. 'That was skill mate, skill: the quickness of the hand deceiving the eye and all that stuff. Anyway, this new idea is not bent either, as you're such a wimp about things like that.'

'You taught me that with your brilliant examples,' I thanked him.

He continued, airily and unruffled. 'As you know, witches and black magic are big business these days, so why don't we do our own video nasty?'

I rolled my eyes as he elaborated, holding his thumb and forefinger up like a frame. 'The Berkeley Witch, Ducker! You remember that story Sutherland told us. What a classic! It's perfect for a video nasty.'

'And a camera? Where do we get one of those?' I asked half-heartedly. He nodded towards the snooker table where Richard Streeter was chalking his cue. He should have been chalking up his 'O' levels but I suppose he'd given them up for a bad job.

'Old man Streeter's got one, hasn't he?'

This was true. He filmed weddings, christenings, summer holidays; the usual boring rubbish people like to look back on when they're bored, to remember for a lifetime. But there was little chance of him lending it to Chico Spielberg, to make a video nasty.

'They're big business, Ducker; legal too, most of them,' he tried to persuade me. 'If we were to charge Swanswell 50p a go – and they'd all want to see it – we would make two hundred in one sitting.'

'And where do we show it? Here? Thornie will love that: all the little kids queueing up to see a video nasty made by other kids.'

'We won't tell him it's a video nasty, will we? We'll call it something posh like . . . media-studies project. And we could show it in the art room, which reminds me. . . .'

And clutching me across my arm he was off to the art room to con Sandy Sanderson into helping 'supervise' this third year art project for us.

The idea was that with teachers 'in charge', old man Streeter would feel quite happy to let us use his JVC. After we'd paid a three hundred pound deposit he felt even happier.

I had to admit this enterprise struck me as even more of a dead loss than all the others put together. But I suppose it was better than sitting round waiting for Noddy's cheque to come bouncing in from the museum, or watching the little bags of cash from Ruthie's gang go piling up in the store-room safe.

The story of the Berkeley Witch gets told to all second years at Swanswell round about Hallowe'en, and it gives them nightmares till Christmas. The old witch was supposed to have sold her soul to the Devil. Just before she died, she asked the family to bury her in a stone coffin – after they'd sewn her up in a stag's skin, of course – secure the coffin lid with iron bolts, bind it with three great chains and place it upright in the church. It had to be watched for three days and nights with prayers and masses said for her soul. Unimpressed by all this however, some demons turned up on the first night and snapped the first chain; more turned up on the second night and snapped chain number two. Then on the third and last night, the Man himself turned up on a black horse to snap the third chain. The coffin lid popped open and the corpse walked towards him. He swept her on to his horse and they rode off into the night with a chorus of terrifying screams.

Not bad as far as local legends go. I must say I'm very thankful not to live next door to the church. Ruthie does, of course.

As Sandy suggested we needed a shooting script, Miss Silverberg, who also seemed quite keen on the idea and had wanted to make a film in the summer term for ages, told him how to set it out – words on one side, directions on the other. Chico, however, is not the greatest kid in the world for setting things down on paper.

'Is this it then?' asked Sandy, shaking the grubby sheet of paper that Chico had pinched out of Stoney's desk. '"Enter crowd with witch's body – dump her in coffin – pray – enter Devil – coffin opens – out jumps witch – gets carried off." That won't last two minutes, let alone twenty.'

'Course it will,' replied Chico as I sniggered in his ear. 'It will if you put in lots of close-ups and gory details. You know: the Devil pulls her head off by accident – that sort of thing. . . .'

Sandy smiled feebly and handed the so-called script past Chico to me; obviously recognising a true genius when he saw one.

Video nasties weren't exactly my style. I'd seen a few; one at Gary's that his parents didn't know about, followed by a rude one that had us all in hysterics; and one at Chico's. It was just the two of us there watching 'Die Screaming' and it was a video that the film company didn't know about either. Anyway, there were quite a few heads rolling in this one, but right at the end, when you think the hero has made it to safety, and he gets in his car to drive away from the burning mansion, a pair of hairy hands grabs him round the neck and the film goes black with the horn still blaring. Fine, except that Chico's brother Dean had come back from the pub unnoticed and chose that moment to tap me on the shoulder.

'Blimey, Ducker,' Chico had complained. 'Do you have to scream like that?'

I could never take them seriously. I mean you have to laugh don't you. I mean you can't laugh and scream at the same time.

Mrs Potter was delighted we were going to make a film, even though she shuddered and said, 'That horrible thing?' when we told her the subject.

'How exactly do you sell your soul to the Devil? Sign a contract?' I asked Davy, another expert on videos, nasty and otherwise. He'd seen *E.T.* on pirate video before Steven Spielberg had even finished making it.

'She do sign his book in her blood,' he suggested, twisting his mouth into a sinister grimace. 'After she have summoned him of course.' 'Summoned him?' I checked, getting the hang of it. 'You mean with all sorts of black magic rituals and things. Dancing naked round the cauldron and that?'

He nodded and we both giggled. But somehow I couldn't see Maria Kelly going that far for us. After all, she'd been chosen for the part because of the acting talent she'd demonstrated playing Elizabeth I in Badger's Summer Fête pageant. I didn't yet know who Chico had in mind for the part of the Devil, but when he told me I didn't think Stoney would go that far for us either. Even he would have been happy seeing us all in hell first.

In the end, guess who landed the plum role? Who round here fancies himself as a cross between Clint Eastwood and Burt Reynolds? Gary wasn't asked to play the part. He *demanded* to play Lucifer. As it was his dad's camera, Chico had to let him. He wore a demon mask, a black cloak made out of the old black-out curtains from Room Three and a pair of horrible hands. He looked as frightening as a Christmas Bazaar!

So, that drama lesson, Chico Spielberg was organising everything out on the field where the light was best. He put a lot of preparation into directing this film and spent the whole of that break painting the word 'Director' on the back of his chair. He had also borrowed a loud-speaker from the sports' department. I was teleplay writer, assistant director, prompter and tea boy. Bonehead was the film crew.

The witch, losing interest already, was standing in front

of her cauldron, a plastic dustbin with some sugar paper round it. Some idiot had daubed the words 'Witch's cauldron' on the side. Sandy had painted a spooky landscape on the sheet: pointed mountains, creepy, weeping willows and a castle with one window lit. This was our scenery, and it was nailed to two posts stretched out behind the witch.

'Right witch, now look horrible and start stirring,' commanded the director. 'And roll 'em!' Bonehead squinted at him through his thick lenses, not moving a muscle. 'Roll 'em, you berk! Start filming I mean!'

At last, message understood, the cameras rolled. The witch of Berkeley rolled her eyes to heaven, shrugged and started to whisk the black stick round the bin like she was beating an egg.

'No, no slower, you dummy – that's supposed to be thick sludge full of newts' eyes and frogs' toes!'

Chico put the loudspeaker on his knee as the witch left the set for a moment, pointed the 'spoon' at his throat and told him if he called her a dummy again he could find himself a new witch – after he'd come out of hospital.

Once again, the witch began to stir the pot, like it was an Irish stew, and Chico at least pretended to be happy with that. 'Right – now cue Devil – cue Devil then!'

Gary, after a prod from me, got up off his chair and leapt into the picture from the wrong side and started to wrestle with the witch. They knocked the cauldron over in their vicious struggle and finally split the backcloth.

'No, no, no! Hold on you idiot! What are you doing?' Chico screamed, much to the delight of the audience who had gathered above by the windows of the science lab behind us.

'She bit my ear!' shouted Gary, still struggling in a mass of tangled black-out curtain and back drop. 'Anyway,' he panted, getting to his cloven hoofs. 'You said I come on and carry her off to hell.'

'That's the last scene, you stupid creep!' shrieked the director, through his loud-speaker. 'At the end you carry her off. This is where you just get her to sign the book. . . .'

Oh yeah, he'd forgotten. Apart from that he'd forgotten to get hold of an old book as well; and as the black cloak draped itself over the director's head, we didn't have a witch any more either.

'May I make a few suggestions,' said Sandy politely. He'd taken his first years outside and was keeping an eye on our epic. 'First, always plan your shot and rehearse it before you actually shoot it. Saves wasting tape for one thing. And also the mike on the camera is picking up everything you scream and shout. So you'll have to stay quiet and indicate what you want by gestures or some-thing. . . .'

Chico squirmed irritably in his chair. The last thing he wanted, having done everything wrong, was to be told how to do it right by someone like Sandy. In the end, like all good directors, he decided to scrap that scene and go on to something else, by which time the bell went for end of lesson. We asked Gonzo if we could miss his maths lesson to make a film and he said of course, provided we came back after school to do the Maths we'd missed. We went to his lesson.

Chico decided to shoot the last and best scene first, with a black horse, supplied by Debbie Sorrell – whose family were half gypsy. We were to shoot it in the old church itself. We had a coffin made specially out of ply-wood, painted grey to look like stone. And some idiot had painted the word 'coffin' on the side. Me, Davy, Beryl and Cheryl were acting as the witch's family and we had to wear black cloaks and hoods, muttering any prayers we could think of, or remember, while Gary Lucifier dragged the witch off. How we were going to get Betty Barge, the stand-in, on the horse, I don't know. Chico was going to do all the shooting himself.

173

The trouble with Betty Barge was that she was fat and round and not remotely witch-like. Maria Kelly, of course, was too realistic. Davy reckoned she'd put a curse on the whole thing after she'd walked out.

When we'd asked the Rev Pendryll for permission to film in the grounds of his church that evening, he didn't seem too keen.

'Well, I suppose so, as long as there's a good Christian message in the end of it all. . . .'

'Oh yes, Reverend,' I assured him, as script writer. 'There is very definitely a very good Christian message at the end.'

Pause. 'Yes . . .? and what exactly is it?'

'Oh . . . er, that if you, er . . . sell your soul to the Devil – he'll come and get you.'

'Hmm. Rather metaphorical,' he sniffed. 'But I suppose it will do.'

Chico hadn't really listened to what Sandy had said about planning his shots or rehearsing them first. Once he'd got all the cast and props assembled round the church door, he started to point his camera.

After telling Chico for the fiftieth time how much the JVC cost and what his dad would do to both of them if it got damaged, Gary finally managed to heave himself on to the horse that Debbie had brought along. Hercules his name was. He was dark brown instead of black and was enormous, but docile. Davy, me and the twins were kneeling down by the church door while the coffin was just inside the porch.

'Action!' the director called and we started to mutter our prayers.

'ACTION!' the director shouted again and we started to gabble our prayers louder and faster. 'I said "action" for goodness' sake!'

'Get moving you gert brute!' shouted Lucifer. 'Hey, he won't flipping budge!'

And a girl in jeans walked calmly on to the set and patted

the horse's rump a couple of times. The horse obeyed and slowly, very slowly, nodded and plodded his way along the path.

'Whoa! Whoa there!' called Gary in an impressive deep voice as the old horse kept nodding and plodding his way towards the church door. Davy and I had to get out of the way fast as giant hooves clopped and clipped on the flagstones we'd been praying on.

'Look scared!' I whispered to Davy.

He was staring curiously at Gary who was leaning back in the saddle at an angle of forty-five degrees and grunting, 'Whoa – stop will you! You stupid gert brute, stop!' And on he went into the low porch knocking his rider off on the way. Debbie had to come to his rescue and rushed forward to grab the bridle of Hercules before he went strolling round the church.

'Cut!' shouted Chico angrily. 'We'll have to edit that lot. Now do the coffin scene!'

We knelt round the coffin with frozen faces of terror as Lucifer strode over the flagstones and pointed at it with a rubber finger.

The coffin shook and vibrated like an old fridge and started to hammer and shout muffled curses. 'Help!' Then it started to rock backwards and forwards as if some great power from Gary's rubber finger was causing all this movement.

I could just make out the muffled curses of 'Help! I'm stuck,' when the coffin tipped over on to its side.

'Great!' shouted Chico. 'Brilliant! Keep going.'

'I do reckon she's in trouble!' peeped Beryl pulling her hood off her head and scaring the audience to death. Mind you there was an awful lot of hammering, banging and shrieking coming from the coffin now. In the end we had to stop filming while we went over to the coffin to get the lid off. It took all of Gary's strength to shift it and a very red, round and breathless Betty Barge popped out like a fat Jack-in-the-Box.

'I nearly suffocated in there, I did! I nearly died, I did! You and your stupid ideas Chico Marks! I'm off home I am!'

What exactly happened next is difficult to say. Whether it was the sight and sound of the angry Witch of Berkeley leaping out of her coffin and shouting at Chico which scared the horse, or a wasp or something, we will never know; but anyway the horse suddenly jerked its head sideways straight into Chico as he was coming forward to intercept Betty. We all stared in horror at the JVC lying on the ground. Even stupid old Hercules was looking at it. For a moment nobody dared speak or move to pick it up. Davy at last broke the spell.

'It bounced off the stones,' he told Chico like he didn't need to.

'I had noticed,' croaked our director with a dry mouth.

'And . . . ooh dear . . . it's rattling,' added Davy, putting his ear to it and shaking it gently but audibly.

'How much did it cost?' Cheryl asked Gary, who was shaking violently.

'You stupid basket,' he hissed like a steam engine, face all red and devilish, even without his mask. 'When our dad finds out. . . .'

'Perhaps it isn't damaged,' I put in. It was.

'Eight hundred quid!' Gary announced clearly. 'Eight hundred quid that camera cost – and that's what you'll be giving me tomorrow morning. . . .'

He snatched the camera from Chico, then with a shudder handed it straight back.

Leaving mask, horrible hands, horns and black cloak scattered over the path, he staggered off in a daze muttering: 'He'll kill me . . . you don't know our dad. That's my stereo gone for a burton . . . my holidays in Spain . . . my new bike . . . all gone now. . . .'

176

For the first time in his life Chico did not know what to say.

'Well, when Noddy gives us his donation tomorrow,' I explained as we packed up solemnly, 'We give Gary the eight hundred and . . . that's all there is to it.'

'Which leaves us with two hundred pound,' said Davy, like he didn't need to. 'And two and a half weeks to go. Run out of money and run out of ideas. You know what that means. . . .'

'Yes,' I muttered very bitterly. 'I know exactly what that means. That everything goes to her over there in the blue corner. . . .'

I jerked my head at the girl in blue dungarees who'd been sitting on the wall watching from a safe distance. She came over as the others wandered off, taking the coffin with them, and started talking to Debbie's horse. Then the two horsey females began to discuss the gymkhana at Rockhampton on Saturday.

'What happened? It all ended rather suddenly, didn't it?' Ruth asked, quite sympathetically for a change. I was so fed up I couldn't even think up any funny remarks for her. So, I told her the whole story. I waited for her to raise her nose and tell me it served me right.

'I don't know,' she sighed sadly, 'this whole thing's getting ridiculous.'

'You said it,' I agreed, liking the tone of her voice. It had lost its bossiness for one thing.

'This money-raising has brought out the worst in all of us,' she confessed out of the blue. 'It's made me self-righteous, arrogant and selfish.'

'You said it,' I encouraged her politely.

'And it's made you even more sly, devious, dishonest and disruptive than before, as well as encouraging all the worst kinds of criminal contacts. Types you were supposed to avoid. . . .'

'Well, anyway,' I coughed modestly to try and shut her up for three seconds. She waited, then with a deep, sagging shrug I said, 'we're finished. All washed up, as they say in films . . . if you want our measly two hundred quid, you're welcome to it. . . .'

'It's not me who wants it, it's for charity,' she had to go and remind me. But that didn't matter any more. It was all over. No more Swimming Pool Appeal and, at last, no more competition with the super-efficient girls. All that remained for me to do was see Noddy and square our account with our executive producer, Mr Streeter.

19. An Unexpected Withdrawal

'I look forward to an immediate improvement'
Mr R. Thorne, Head

'What d'you mean there's a problem?' I yelped at Noddy, our saviour, as we surrounded him in Room Two.

'Well, it's old Farmer Gilpin not me,' he explained, backing himself into a corner. 'He did come round to our house last night, banging on the door and wanting to know what I was up to. . . .'

This was after the museum had rung him up to ask for permission to explore his land for further remains. They had to tell him about the sword, and how much it was worth, but the minute he realised it was going to Noddy Bright he hit the farmhouse roof. He'd really sent Noddy down to the fields by the shore to stop him poking about the farmyards, we all knew that.

'But he now reckons he knew about the treasure all along and just sent me to find it for him and that we promised to share it,' Noddy continued, ears pink with outrage. 'He says he's going to take it to court and everything.'

'He can't do that. You found it, it's yours,' shouted Davy. 'Ain't that right, Ducker?' I knew nothing about Treasure Trove so said nothing.

'If he does take it to court you won't see your money for ages,' Chico groaned. 'Then you'll spend it all on lawyers' fees.'

'You could always ask Ruthie for a loan,' Davy suggested. To my amazement he was being serious. There was a long pause with everybody looking at everybody else for a solution. Chico stood hands in pockets whistling quietly at the ceiling. Then suddenly he patted me cheerfully on the cheeks.

'Never mind, Ducker old son, you'll think of something,' he reassured me, backing out of the door and waving the team good-bye. There they all were, staring at me waiting for me to think of something: Davy, Beryl and Cheryl, Noddy and Bonehead.

'We could always start again, Ducker,' grunted Bonehead behind his finger. The rest all nodded eagerly, except Davy this time. I shook my head.

'Look team, let me say this,' I began manfully. I looked at Noddy still pink with frustration. 'Er . . . Nigel, thanks for the treasure, but if I were you, I should keep the lot. We don't deserve it, I mean I don't. And you Stephen . . .' I turned to Bonehead calling him by his proper name for the first and last time. 'I know I've been a bit tight on you sometimes, taking the mick and everything, but . . . you've done a great job and you've been really loyal, you know . . . so thanks . . . but forget it from now on.'

He looked really chuffed and blushed behind his thick lenses.

'I know I've been a little bighead sometimes,' I confessed.

'Sometimes?' echoed Davy mischievously.

'But you've all been great, far better than I deserved, so. . . .'

This was really turning out to be a sad moment. I was almost in tears. I had nothing much left to say to anybody now. I just thrust my hands in my pockets and stared mournfully at the holes in my sneakers. When I heard the soft patter of applause I thought for a moment that somebody was being sarcastic. Had Chico nipped back for a quick laugh? But when I turned to the doorway there stood three girls.

We all gaped as the three of them came striding purpose-fully through the door: Ruth, with the gorgeous Dawn on one side of her and the delicious Lucy Gillimore on the other.

'C'mon, Ducker, don't be down-hearted, we've decided to help you out,' she announced and took my arm. 'We shall lend you the three hundred. . . .'

'With interest of course,' Dawn added with a cool, calculating smile. 'We'll go and get Des to open the safe for us right now.'

She certainly timed it well. I wondered what her angle was, if there was one, but there wasn't time to bow or kiss her boots. On the way down the corridor I told her what a truly wonderful person she was.

'Save the grovelling for Thornie,' Ruth reprimanded me in mid-grovel. They had to frog-march to the office to hurry me up, and there I waited obediently.

With about five minutes to go before the end of break they came trotting up to me moaning that they couldn't find Des anywhere. Mrs Franklin told us he hadn't been seen all day. The last time the girls had seen him was at half-past four yesterday afternoon when he'd cashed some money raised by their pathetic Sponsored Spell. Still, they had totalled five hundred and eighty two pounds. Mrs Franklin took the key down from the wall and went into the store room to unlock the safe.

'He's probably got a hangover,' I told them, knowing that he and Sandy were quite fond of the amber liquid. He even dared ask my dad once if he could have a drink on tick. Dad said he'd pretend he hadn't heard the question – then after Des had slunk off, promptly told everyone what he'd just heard.

'Are you sure they money was in here?' We heard Mrs F's voice call out to us from the store room. We turned to see her huge behind scarcely framed by the black safe.

'Two separate bags,' Ruth told her without a trace of concern.

'Can't see them now,' the reply pointed out. Next thing she knew, three girls were pushing her out of the way and ransacking the safe, then the store room.

'It must be here somewhere!' Dawn gasped. I waited for the right moment to tell them. When at last it dawned on her and the other two that the thousand pounds worth of loot had indeed gone; that is, had been nicked, – there was a great scrum in the corridor followed by various phone-calls and Mr Thorne himself was on the scene, looking as confused and bewildered as anybody else.

The first thing he did was to send the girls and me back to our lesson. Can't think why, just because the bell had gone ten minutes ago.

'Try Dinah Spargo,' I told Ruth. 'She's bound to know where Des is.'

We sprinted to the art room where Sandy was setting up some models for his fourth years. But there was no sign of Dinah Spargo. Sandy who never knew what was going on, which kids were supposed to be in, and which kids were supposed to be out, went up to the sixth form room to check. Meanwhile the fourth year gossip shop was leaning up against the art room cupboard. I picked up a clip board and hiding behind it crept as close as I could.

'They never – they must be flipping cracked!'

'They did – last night, her mum said.'

'What she want to leave a note for. Give it all away. They'll go and catch her now. . . .'

'Guilty conscience about her mum, I reckon. . . .'

'Yeah – but what they going to live on? How they going to afford the plane fare, I ask you?'

'They don't have to go on flipping Concorde. It's only a couple of hundred . . . I admire her meself. It takes guts to do something like that.'

'Guts? Nuts more like it. Her and Grisewald? I ask you. They're both nuts!'

'That'll be one in the eye for Ruthie Pendryll.'

'Yeah, she didn't half fancy him. . . .'

He'd nicked our money to buy plane tickets to elope with Dinah Spargo to the US of A – that was all. Thornie must have been dead embarrassed; after all, he's the one who gave him the job. Everybody round the school was stunned, especially the girls and one girl in particular.

'I-I just can't believe it,' she kept saying over and over again, after PC Blackwood had interviewed her and the rest of us in Thornie's office. 'I mean, running off with a sex-mad sixth-former is one thing . . . but to steal our money. . . .'

'No wonder he was so keen on helping us beat Ducker's mob,' said Dawn emptily.

'No wonder he wanted it kept in the school safe and not in the bank, like I suggested,' Lucy put in wisely, now that it was too late.

There was only one question left for me to ask Ruth, and as the others walked off down the corridor ahead of us I saw my chance.

'You didn't really fancy that creep did you?'

'No,' she retorted with a funny sort of rise at the end of the word. So I told her all about the interesting little conversation I'd overheard with Shane Delroy the Radio DJ in the pub garden. I had to spice it up a bit of course. And the romance by the Pill, Davy and I had seen.

'Well if you knew all that,' she snapped, 'why didn't you warn me earlier? This is all your fault. . . .'

All my fault? I choked back all the insults and obscenities that were queueing up, swallowed them and, staying cool, saying nothing, smiled to myself. After all, she had offered to save us, her arch enemy and that must have taken a big effort on her part. Plus the fact that she'd just had her heart broken and could therefore be forgiven if she was bitter about everyone and everything.

20. The End of a
Song and Dance

*Parents' comments: Although my husband and I are
deeply disappointed in this term's report, we both have
faith in the staff's ability to remedy the problem.*

They found Dinah first. She came back alone and gave
herself up at New York airport, presumably disillusioned,
as the newspaper report in Dad's *Guardian* said she knew
nothing about the theft. He, on the other hand, got as far as
California, having spent all his money, and all of ours. The
report also mentioned that, despite suspicions, he didn't
have a stolen video camera either, or know anything about
it.

'Who told the police Grisewald nicked the video
camera?' I asked Chico the day before the barn dance. He,
would you believe, had no idea. But, as he pointed out, it
let us off the hook. Streeter was bound to have it insured.

'So . . . where's the camera now?' I checked. He looked
surprised. It had to be him.

'A mate of Dean's reckons he can repair it – just,' Chico
said chirpily, being in the brightest of moods.

'And when he repairs it he'll give it back to you to find
again to give back to Gary.'

'Sure, if you insist,' he agreed quite readily. 'At least it
saves you the fuss of finding eight hundred quid. The things
I do for you, Ducker.'

Noddy managed to get all the money that was due to him
and Gilpin refused to let the museum dig up his field, he
was so angry. His old mum was very pleased, though, and
so was her new stepfather, who wasn't all that well-off but a

darn sight nicer than his real father. Badger organised a humanities trip one afternoon to go down to Bristol and see this magnificent rusty old sword and brooch that our saviour had found; and very nice they looked too, especially as it made a change from an afternoon's school work.

As for me, I was just glad it was all over. I had devoted three whole weeks of my life to that stupid appeal; half my time spent trying to raise money, and the other half hiding from the consequences.

Thornie had planned this barn-dance for that last Saturday of term as a sort of grand finale and knees-up and he called it a Ceilidh. Not a bad idea really, except that the Swanswell Street Theatre had to put in a guest appearance. Loads of mums and dads were there; some courageous locals; even some teachers who had dared to bring their wives along. My mother was there, being very keen on ceilidhs and things like that. Spencer Burroughs helped Mrs Stone on the hot-dog stand, looking very pleased with himself too.

A Ceilidh, or barn-dance, means that a bloke stands on the stage with a microphone shouting out commands, while this great musical scrum dances clumsily into and out of itself round the yard in front of him. I spent most of my time apologising; either for getting the steps wrong or stepping on somebody else's.

Anyway, half-way through the long, warm summer evening with the house-martins hunting gnats over our heads or watching the show from their balconies under the guttering, Davy got on the small stage and managed to juggle for nine seconds; Donna and Shane, the amazing acrobatic dog, had the audience 'aahing' and applauding for ten seconds, especially when he headed the balloon; Benny juggled with his rats and I sat painfully on a shaky stool with Beryl on one knee and Cheryl on the other.

'Tell me, Pickles,' I said, giving the doll a brisk shake.

'What goes black and white and black and white and black and white?'

'A sunburnt penguin? Ooh no, that's the other one,' she shrieked. Not again I thought.

'So what's black and white and red all over?' I asked Cheese. Would you believe it, she'd forgotten. But the audience shouted the punch line out for her. They'd all had a few jars of beer, or scrumpy from the huge barrel wallowing in the servery so they were in the right mood and had a good laugh. When Beryl-pudding started to shiver with giggles they laughed even more.

Jammy, once again, was the star of the show, playing a magical medley from *Cats*, then half a dozen Irish jigs. Old man McMenemy managed to control himself during the first five, but the last one had him on his feet.

'That's me boy!' he yelled and started to dance his dainty jig in the middle of the yard, to the embarrassment of his wife and six kids watching. But the jars of beer and scrumpy did their job once more and several others thought 'what the heck' and joined in, until everybody was dancing and twirling themselves around, doing their own thing to Jammy's Jig as it started to go on for as long as a symphony. Thornie was obviously enjoying himself. Even when he came to ask me where Chico was, he still had a broad grin on his face.

'I thought you said he had an act as well?'

He realised what my stammering, stumbling answers meant and went looking for him. I followed Thornie's search closely round the back of the gym to see Chico and his table and ball and cups about to perform his little act for the members of the band who were enjoying their break.

'Now I normally charge 50p a time, but seeing as it's you lot, I shall only ask you for a quid, then all you do is tell me where the white ball is because now it's under the blue cup but I move the blue cup just a little bit and the blue cup's between the, er . . . other two . . . and hello Mister Thorne, what a lovely evening. . . .'

He stood left foot on right foot as Thornie peered over his shoulder down at the table, paused, pounced and lifted the ball between forefinger and thumb.

'I prefer this version,' he said holding the ball close to Chico's face. 'I take the little white ball and insert it in your left ear.'

'Oh no, sir, that would be far too easy . . . wouldn't it?' Chico gulped. 'No, because you will have disappeared, along with your little table and little cups, understand?'

He understood. He packed up and later leaned against the gym wall sulking, until he eventually joined in and found that barn dances weren't at all the boring rubbish he'd said they were. Soon he was taking great pleasure in trying to swing Maria Kelly round in some dangerous manoeuvre called a 'basket'.

I seemed to keep bumping into Ruth through the course of the various dances. Miss Bleach was clinging on to Sandy in a desperate attempt at making Thornie jealous. Thornie was dancing with everybody, and talking to everybody else in between. My mother talked to him, but they were soon both laughing so it must have been all right. Then Thornie was talking to Miss Bleach, who never laughed but on this occasion managed to smile graciously.

'What suddenly made you change your mind about the challenge?' I asked Ruth as we took a break. 'You know, the money-raising?'

'Someone high up put in a good word for you,' she said as Thornie staggered over to rest on a bale of straw.

'You mean God?' I teased blasphemously.

'No, chump – Thornie!'

'Mister Thorne, if you don't mind, Ruthie. That's no way to speak of our glorious leader . . . whom all the children love and admire. . . .'

She gave me a funny glance and shuddered. 'You sound like Miss Bleach.'

Talk of the devil; the man himself came up behind up and put his arms round us both. The smell of warm beer wafted over us like a Sahara wind. 'And how are my favourite third years?' he chortled cheerfully. 'Signed the peace treaty yet?'

Ruth smiled awkwardly, at him not at me. 'We're still negotiating, sir,' I told him.

'Very wise,' he exclaimed, ruffling my hair, something I hated. 'After all you can't be too careful with this character you know; I mean he is borderline. . . .'

And before he could blurt out any more rubbish, he was collared by a rosy-cheeked Miss Bleach who called him 'Bobby' and wanted him for the next dance. Ruth sipped her orange squash and frowned thoughtfully. Then this fat little bearded bloke got up behind his microphone and began to bellow beerily at us to 'Take your partners!'

'What did he mean by that, "borderline"?' she asked suddenly as we got up to dance. She made it sound as if I was gay or something.

'No idea,' I grunted loudly. 'Yet another of his great mysteries. . . .'

'Mysteries? What's that supposed to mean?' she gasped, well and truly confused. 'What's he been up to? Don't destroy my last illusion for God's sake.'

First me, then Des Grisewald and now Thornie. No wonder she was panicking. But for someone who didn't want her illusions shattered she certainly asked a lot of questions. And I realised I'd said too much. The worst thing you can do with a girl is tell her you know a secret and then try and keep it a secret. One way or other, she'll wheedle it out of you. . . .

'Come on, what's all this about?' she wheedled desperately.

'It's just our little joke about going into 'O' level classes,' I lied. 'He keeps teasing me about being borderline CSE so I work harder.'

'Oh is that all?' she groaned, disappointed more than relieved.

And so the dance went on dancing until midnight. The band drove off in a battered mini van; Thornie was shaking hands and embracing people shouting 'Good night Mr This, and Goodnight Mrs That,' loud enough to wake all the surrounding villagers. Gnats gathered invisibly in the cooling air to ambush us as we crossed the car-park. And Ruthie saw me safely home.

We got our swimming pool in the end, the boring way. The water was freezing cold and started to leak out after the first few weeks, and we're still waiting for it to be repaired. But I have better things to occupy myself with: eight 'O' levels and one CSE in fund-raising to start with. But it was all worth it though; I mean, at least I learned how to swim.

*You can see more from Teens
on the following pages:*

A selected list of titles available from Teens · Mandarin

While every effort is made to keep prices low, it is sometimes necessary to increase prices at short notice. Teens · Mandarin reserve the right to show new retail prices on covers which may differ from those previously advertised in the text or elsewhere.

The prices shown below were correct at the time of going to press.

☐	416 06252 0	**Nick's October**	Alison Prince	£1.95
☐	416 06232 6	**Haunted**	Judith St George	£1.95
☐	416 08082 0	**The Teenagers Handbook**	Murphy/Grime	£1.95
☐	416 08822 8	**The Changeover**	Margaret Mahy	£1.95
☐	416 06242 3	**I'm Not Your Other Half**	Caroline B. Cooney	£1.95
☐	416 08572 5	**Rainbows of the Gutter**	Rukshana Smith	£1.95
☐	416 03202 8	**The Burning Land**	Siegel/Siegel	£1.95
☐	416 03192 7	**Survivors**	Siegel/Siegel	£1.95
☐	416 09672 7	**Misfits**	Peggy Woodford	£1.95
☐	416 12022 9	**Picture Me Falling In Love**	June Foley	£1.95
☐	416 04022 5	**Fire and Hemlock**	Diana Wynne Jones	£1.95
☐	416 09232 2	**Short Cut to Love**	Mary Hooper	£1.95
☐	416 13102 6	**Frankie's Story**	Catherine Sefton	£1.99
☐	416 13922 1	**All the Fun of the Fair**	Anthony Masters	£1.99

All these books are available at your bookshop or newsagent, or can be ordered direct from the publisher. Just tick the titles you want and fill in the form below.

Teens · Mandarin Paperbacks, Cash Sales Department, PO Box 11, Falmouth, Cornwall TR10 9EN.

Please send cheque or postal order, no currency, for purchase price quoted and allow the following for postage and packing:

UK — 55p for the first book, 22p for the second book and 14p for each additional book ordered to a maximum charge of £1.75.

BFPO and Eire — 55p for the first book, 22p for the second book and 14p for each of the next seven books, thereafter 8p per book.

Overseas Customers — £1.00 for the first book plus 25p per copy for each additional book.

NAME (Block Letters) ....

ADDRESS ....

....